Cyberpunk as you've never seen it before…

Science fiction is all about outrageous ideas. Nice Malay girls breaking the rules. Censorship. Brain drain. Moral policing. Migrant exploitation. All the stuff of fiction, obviously.

But these 14 short stories take it one step further. The nice Malay girls are cyborgs. The spambots are people. The brains have drained into cyberspace, and the censorship is inside your head.

Welcome to **Cyberpunk: Malaysia**.

FIXI NOVO manifesto

1. We believe that omputih/gwailoh-speak is a Malaysian language.

2. We use American spelling. This is because we are more influenced by Hollywood than the House of Windsor.

3. We publish stories about the urban reality of Malaysia. If you want to share your grandmother's World War 2 stories, send 'em elsewhere and you might even win the Booker Prize.

4. We specialize in pulp fiction, because crime, horror, sci-fi and so on turn us on.

5. We will not use italics for non-American/ non-English terms. This is because those words are not foreign to a Malaysian audience. So we will not have "They had *nasi lemak* and went back to *kongkek*" but rather "They had nasi lemak and went back to kongkek". Nasi lemak and kongkek are some of the pleasures of Malaysian life that should be celebrated without apology; italics are a form of apology.

6. We publish novels and short-story anthologies. We don't publish poetry; we like making money.

7. The existing Malaysian books that come closest to what we wanna do: *Devil's Place* by Brian Gomez; and the Inspector Mislan crime novels by Rozlan Mohd Noor. Look for them!

8. We publish books with the same print run and the same price as those of our parent company, Buku Fixi. So a book of about 300 pages will sell at RM20. This is because we wanna reach out to the young, the sengkek and the kiam siap.

CALL FOR ENTRIES.

Interested? For novels,
send your synopsis and first 2 chapters.
For anthologies, send a short story of between 2,000-5,000 words on the theme "KL Noir."
Send to **info@fixi.com.my** anytime.

CYBERPUNK: MALAYSIA

EDITED BY

ZEN CHO

Published by
Fixi Novo *which is an imprint of:*
Buku Fixi (002016254-V)
B-8-2A Opal Damansara, Jalan PJU 3/27
47810 Petaling Jaya, Malaysia
info@fixi.com.my
http://fixi.com.my

Cyberpunk: Malaysia

Editor: Zen Cho

First Printing: June 2015

Cover and layout: Teck Hee
Consultant: Alyssa Mohamad

ISBN 978-967-0750-87-3
Catalogue-in-Publication Data available from the National Library of Malaysia.

Printed by:
Vinlin Press Sdn Bhd
2 Jalan Meranti Permai 1, Meranti Permai Industrial Park
Batu 15, Jalan Puchong, 47100 Puchong, Malaysia

WHAT YOU WILL FIND IN THIS BOOK:

For an idea of what 133t-speak sounded like IRL, go to the Arkib Elektronika on Jalan Usah Nama and look up a dial-up modem. Audio samples are also available on the website. *(page 30)*

"Eighty strokes for possession of a can of beer?" she said incredulously. *(page 50)*

Perhaps it was time to get a fully hands-free one; there was only so long she could get away with pretending to be deliberately retro, instead of admitting that she just couldn't afford the upgrade. *(page 70)*

"My name is Yachoba Maru, a deposed Crown Prince from Nigeria. I wish to transfer overseas the amount of seven million dollars to – " *(page 95)*

Once initiated, the fractal algorithm organizes the base blocks into specialized tools.The most basic is the Picoweaver (ranging from 50 to 300 picometers in maximum length). *(page 108)*

Everyone knew that the best andromaids were made in China. Chinese andromaids were smart, loyal and efficient. Their batteries lasted forever and they were mostly maintenance free. *(page 117)*

"Do you not understand that we cannot remain here like this, always running and following orders? This is not how one should live." *(page 149)*

She had no idea how many kilometers it was from the border crossing at Su Ngai Ko Lok to the crossing at Padang Besar, but she knew it wasn't going to be a leisurely stroll through the woods. *(page 171)*

"Don't disturb the barrier. You want to be ABC? Ever had ABC? Never mind – sit! You want to die, is it?" *(page 194)*

He picked up a walking stick that was leaning against the wall of the hut. Closing his eyes, he brought it down on the old man's head. *(page 222)*

"Complete system failure. Complete system failure." *(page 251)*

In its heart, it is rumored, lies the Titiwangsa Lake; there are no records of what the lake looks like now, only grainy videos of doubtful veracity made by urban explorers. *(page 272)*

Terror – not meaning horror, but the word used in its celebratory sense, somebody seeing a burning piece, or a cool perspective-trick painting, and saying: "Wah, so terror!" *(page 287)*

I was so emo remembering my dad bringing me to OldTown for their premixed coffees and freshly microwaved nasi lemaks. *(page 306)*

CONTENTS

INTRO

What is it with Malaysians and nostalgia? Even our science fiction looks to the past: William Gibson's classic cyberpunk novel *Neuromancer* was published in 1984, before the editor was even born.

There is something almost quaint in the idea of cyber superconsciousnesses and hackers fighting the Man in our era of Instagram, iPhones and Internet surveillance as an accepted fact of life.

But science fiction is always more about the era that produced it than the actual future that followed. Golden Age SF was about the Cold War; cyberpunk was about the '80s and '90s. Science fiction is about the culture that produced it, too—mostly American (though sometimes British).

So what is the Malaysian cyberpunk of 2015 about?

Unsurprisingly, religion and politics (and religion *as* politics) are front and center. Still, the head covering in Angeline Woon's *Underneath Her Tudung* is less there to make a religious point than as a social nicety. Nice Malay girls wear tudung, and if MMU-Model DN-01152 doesn't wear hers, people might realize she's a cyborg.

What nice Malay girls are allowed—and not allowed—is the driver of Anna Tan's *Codes*, in which what you are able to access on the Internet is governed by your identity. Etiquette in a world overwhelmed by social media is explored in *Personal* by Sharmilla Ganesan, and Terence Toh runs with that the theme to the point of absurdity in *Attack of the Spambots*.

ONE HUNDRED YEARS: Machine by Rafil Elyas and *What the Andromaid Reads at Night* by Ted Mahsun address religion more directly. Each envisions a different end of the spectrum a cyberpunk Malaysia could end up on, though funnily enough, in both versions of the future, divergences from orthodoxy are strictly policed by the authorities. Our religious sentiments may change—but political repression we will ever have with us.

The marks of migrant labour and economic inequality are also stamped on the anthology, as they are in the homes and on the streets of modern urban Malaysia. *KAKAK* by William Tham Wai Liang speculates about how we would treat robot laborers. Kris Williamson's cynical response in *The Wall That Wasn't A Wall* suggests that the answer may be, "Not much better than humans—but also not much worse."

Adiwijaya Iskandar's *The Twins* starts with a pair of siblings on the run in a strangely transformed, strangely familiar landscape dominated by the ruins of twin towers (a specter that appears in more than one story). In Chin Ai-May's *October 11*, it's also in the transformed "no man's land" of KL that an exile strives to recover his memories.

The examination of the unreliability of our minds—and their potential—continues in the next two stories, which take place in the now-familiar setting of a KL architecturally and administratively divided into haves and have-nots. In *Undercover in Tanah Firdaus* by Tina Isaacs, a representative of the ruling elite reconsiders his preconceptions of the poor. In Tariq Kamal's *Unusual Suspects*, the perspective moves again from the powerful to the outcast, focusing on the power of the apparently humble to subvert the great.

And the anthology ends, appropriately, on that note of subversion: both *The White Mask* by Zedeck Siew and Foo Sek Han's *Extracts from DMZINE #13 (January 2115)* are about revolution. Clear-eyed as they are about our nation's failings, they are also optimistic about the potential for our art and creativity and plain old stubbornness to save us.

I've drawn out the themes I saw in the 14 vibrant, interesting stories that make up *Cyberpunk: Malaysia*, but what you will find when you read the stories is that they are never just about one thing—just as there is never only one perspective on anything in Malaysia. They embody the complexity of our flawed and fascinating country, as well as both the critique and reluctant optimism of the best SF. They are also a ton of fun. I hope you enjoy them.

Zen Cho
London, May 2015

Underneath Her Tudung

×

ANGELINE WOON

"Apa tu? Robot? Hihihi…If robots can become doctors, then anything can become doctors. Kereta pun boleh. Seterika pun boleh. Sudu garpu pun boleh jadi doktor!"

—Minister of Health and Consumer Affairs at the groundbreaking ceremony of the MMU robotics factory, Genting Jaya, 2051

"Got you."

I tried to stuff my hair back under the tudung but received a small jolt of electricity for my trouble.

"Ow."

The nanocable conglomerate, free once more from my effort to imprison them, swayed gently against my forehead. I swear they were laughing at me. The optical sensors at the end of the nanocables were lit a gentle blue.

What lah. I needed help. I pinged Ah Weng and had to wait 2.46 seconds for his image to pop up over my vid feed.

"Hi, Doc," said Ah Weng, yawning. Poor guy was up all night running last-minute system checks on my software. "How's the first day back on the job?"

"I'm having a bad hair day. Fix it."

"I'm your mechanic lah, not your hairdresser."

"Ah *Weng*…"

"Okay, okay…I still can't do anything. Soli! The nanocables get their instructions locally."

"Meaning?"

"Meaning all directions come from your nervous system. I can't do anything from here. Drop in after your shift for servicing and see how lah."

Great. So this rebellion by my hair meant I was subconsciously trying to secede from myself.

As I pondered getting a crew cut, a shadow loomed over me. It belonged to a member of the Unit Pengesan Maksiat. We called them maks for obvious reasons. The man glared at me with the Official Face, the kind that could only have come from sucking the life out of the mother of all limau puruts. It took real training, that face.

"Mana IC? Mana AC?"

Fulawei. Identity card and bank account number at one go.

He looked me up and down, most likely calculating the surface area of black jubah per volume of tempting flesh that I carried about on sinful bones. I'd seen that look before, usually with other women as targets. With much regret, I realized that I'd never before said or done anything to mitigate such odiousness. To correct that error, I asked:

"Isn't account-checking the domain of the Unit Pencegah Jenayah?"

Maks never liked comparisons to the Jens. The Jens were the prime movers, the darlings, the boss of all law enforcement branches of the Genting Jaya Group (GJG on the shiny badges, Jijik to the wits in private), the current, and only, corporation that ran the Federation of Malaysia. Maks tended to be washouts from the Jen program, hence their attitude.

The mak's smile glowed like the surface of a well-seasoned wok. "In case you didn't know, Cik, this is Genting Jaya, capital city of the Federation of Malaysia. The rakyat who want to live here must be pious. I have to check all suspicious, potentially sinful activity, Cik."

"Good boy. Thanks for the Geografi and Pendidikan Moral lesson," I said, and got up to leave. The mak blocked my exit, and, when I tried to sidestep, shoved his force-stick against my chest.

"Mana IC? Mana AC?"

Fed up, I grabbed the wrist holding the weapon and pushed it away. He tried to pull free, but my left arm was a souped-up part of me—mechanical, cybernetic, hard as steel and soft as synthskin™. His expression turned from one of unfulfilled desire into anger.

Still holding his wrist, I waved my other hand in front of his face to make sure he paid attention. Despite the drain on my batteries, I activated the most accurate, high-resolution version of my identity module. The hologram of the mobius strip keris hovered brightly over my palm in the harsh sunlight.

"You're Group?" he croaked. I nodded at my colleague.

The hologram switched mid-swirl to that of a spiky buckyball. His eyes widened in fear. Even maks feared members of the Unit Pengesan Virus. With the blink of an eye, I could label him a Sickie and send him into permanent quarantine under the dome in Kuala Lumpur.

"Puas?" I asked.

He nodded vigorously in response. "Terima kasih, Cik... Puan...Tuan. Terima kasih."

My hair jabbed him between the eyes.

He screamed, "What are you?" before clamping his mouth shut with his free hand. My God, I thought I would have to deal with a cardiac arrest there and then.

I ignored his question and wrote him an MC for the afternoon off, since he looked like he was in a state of shock. Padan muka.

He thanked me again before running away like hantu were at his heels. White coat syndrome? Cyborg-phobia? Or maybe he thought I was a late-model penanggal?

Ah Weng pinged me with a patient's chart. The moment I accepted the case, a countdown timer was activated, showing I had twelve minutes to get to my patient. The X-spot app mapped my route in 3D, then flattened to a virtual yellow line overlaying the physical road ahead. I ran where the yellow line told me to go.

I received a live audio-visual feed from Ah Weng. Official some more.

"I hereby notify you that you've been given a black mark on your file," he said. I grunted.

A text message came over our secret, and hopefully secure, line. Ah Weng again. He piggybacked the text messages on the official audio-visual feed so that the higher-ups wouldn't know we were conferring in private. I replied as I ran (don't worry, I am a trained professional).

MechaBss: Shouldn't have done that wor. Made an enemy of him.

Cyberdoc: He shouldn't have touched me.

MechaBss: Just doing his job what. Also, Unit Pengesan Virus? Blatant misrepresentation.

Cyberdoc: Ya meh? Should I hand in my consultant badge?

MechaBss: No lah. But Dee? Cannot just mengamuk like war robot, okay?

Cyberdoc: Cheh.

The main problem with being a Mobile Medical Unit was that people thought you wanted to shoot people all the time instead of save lives. MMUs are not war robots. They were developed during the Virus pandemic in Kuala Lumpur. Death toll among frontliners was high, both from the virus and from the chaos that had descended upon the afflicted city, so robots were created to treat and police the city folk. After the dome quarantine was enforced, the Group kept up its MMU fleet rather than dismantle the expensive operation.

Unfortunately, the robots were lousy peacetime doctors. They couldn't empathize with patients. To save the program, the Group merged robots with human doctors, ostensibly for their bedside manners. Most of the chosen doctors had suffered from terminal illnesses or injuries from accidents. Others had been persuaded, via threats or pretty promises, to climb into the metal suit. One foolish girl volunteered. For a decade, MMUs have technically been cyborgs, but the Group, for bizarre reasons of its own, passed them off as robots.

I was one of those disguised cyborgs.

Life as a faux-robot is no fun. For one thing, they wiped our memories so we could function better as robots. Crazy, right? Why even bother with the human element? Just write a better robot software or something. But that's Genting Jaya for you.

Due to a blip in my programming, I had flashbacks to my former life. Ah Weng was tasked to fix me, which he did, by rebooting to default. Ta-daa! Human again. Mostly. About 44.67 percent organic, and really, the brain counted for more than mere spare parts, didn't it? At least, that was what I liked to tell myself in the dark of night.

The steady jogging calmed me down enough to realize that any black mark against me went against Ah Weng too. In the Group, we're all team members—huzzah!

Cyberdoc: Sorry about our KPI.

MechaBss: Is okay. The look on his face? Worth it.

Cyberdoc: Hang on. How you know?

MechaBss: Your hair sent me a shot.

I laughed, but inwardly I felt disturbed. The look of horror on the mak's face…

I kept running. The refrain "What are you?" thudded in my mind in the wake of my footfalls.

A short while later I came to a screeching halt. Gears clanked, the suspension squeaked (high-grade konon) as my weight settled and coolant leaked in soft hisses under my clothes. It was embarrassing, but I had other worries.

"Ah Weng, do you see what I see, in this most eventful place, this fine city of ours coruscating atop the cool ridges of the Banjaran Titiwangsa?"

The mechanic whistled as he watched the feed I sent him. "Jam giler."

All about me the masses milled. They waved tokens of gratitude, gleaned during their observation of the holy hour. They lined up at the many AmKedai booths, talking excitedly, catching up with news from the jiran tetangga, letting their children run wild, screaming.

"Jam giler," I agreed. "You're the guy with the scientific calculator. You're zen with GPS. You're one with the atomic clock. So why didn't you factor in that it's makan time in the Souk?"

"The Souk? What are you doing there? Hang on, let me check."

MechaBss: Dee. That's not the X-spot path I sent you!!!!!

Cyberdoc: Aiks! Kena sabo! Better pretend it was the right file for now.

"Nope, nothing wrong with the X-spot file," said Ah Weng out loud. "In fact, it's the best route we got."

MechaBss: Die. All other possible paths have temporary roadblocks and detours. We're being targeted.

Cyberdoc: Gee. I'm starting to think the bosses hate us.

MechaBss: We always knew they'd come for revenge because I didn't mindwipe you when the flashbacks started.

Cyberdoc: Come to think, why didn't you?

MechaBss: Kaypoh lor. Other cyborgs if got problems they would cincai reinstall the OS, but they sent you to me for special treatment. I wanted to know who you were.

Mana tau you're Atasan!

Cyberdoc: Not me. I work for a living. You're talking about Dian's mother.

MechaBss: Dee. You are Dian.

Cyberdoc: Save the psychoanalysis for later. I'm on the job.

MechaBss: Righty-ho. You the boss.

Cyberdoc: Sorry, Weng. That was out of line. Look, Mother's influence may have kept me from the scrap heap, and your development of self-programming cybernetics is your saving grace, but there are all kinds of ways for the bosses to make life miserable for us.

MechaBss: Tell me about it. My paperwork got bumped down last week for missing one comma. Leceh.

Cyberdoc: Ah Weng. Serious lah. If our KPI drops too much they can kick us out of the MMU program.

MechaBss: Okay. Serious? I have no illusions of the danger we're in. They may find another genius, and accidents can happen. But I think it'll take some time, so we're safe for now. Let's just do our jobs, like you said, and talk later. Generic malt drinks are on you, Cyberdoc.

Cyberdoc: That's a promise, MechaBss. Thanks.

Ramlee Souk was a dilapidated, ancient kawasan, with buildings dating back to before the founding of Genting Jaya. Everything else after that had been built higgledy-piggledy in every nook and cranny of the highlands, some downward like the west end of the Atasan Tower, and some extending outward from the cliffs, like the Singapore sector. The resulting mess meant that most 3D maps of the area looked like they came from a protein modeling software.

In the rest of Genting Jaya, a man might decide to visit a neighbor, who, despite being in an adjacent flat, actually lives in another building. The man might have to go up a floor, and up again on another stairwell, then down a floor, and down again using escalators. He'd have to negotiate tingkats and arases and stories (there were no standards in nomenclature), now going left, then right, then left and right again, through multiple tunnels, corridors and moving sidewalks. He might walk from the concourse of Bangunan A straight to the roof of Bangunan B before reaching his friend's place. But if he lived in the Ramlee Souk, all he would have to do is go to Aras 1, negotiate the main market area to his friend's building, then ride the lift up to his friend's floor.

The trick was getting through Aras 1, which was, as I surveyed it, chock-a-block with humanity. Pushing through the crowd brought back a muscle memory, a flashback of wading in the sea. Had I really done that before? Not recently, and not as MMU-Model DN-01152. It had to be Dian. Privileged Dian, daughter of the Atasan, a class of people so high up they controlled the Group. She never had a day's worry and could afford to go to the seaside. Idealistic Dian, who signed up for the cyborg fleet just so she could get away from her guilt of being born with a silver spoon in her mouth.

A little girl ran into me and clutched my legs.

"Don't want ekonoMi. Yucks," she screamed. "Want MmmMmmMmm..."

I looked around for a parental unit, but saw no one who seemed to want the child back. Meanwhile, the tantrum drew disgusted looks and comments about my terrible parenting skills. Dian Yusoff had had a daughter. What would she do?

I picked up the child and tried to comfort her, but she kept crying. Even my hair got in the act with a quiet but complex light show, but the girl's eyes were screwed tightly shut so she missed all the fun.

"Haish, sorry, Cik. Come here, Ana, don't disturb people," said a harried adult who was carrying a basket full of plain ekonoMi containers. No pre-Mi-Mmm for this family. There was nothing nutritionally different between the two, though the premium stuff, I'd been told, tasted better. I was never able to tell the difference. Atasan Dian, I reminded myself, never had cause to eat the stuff.

The mother reached us and I passed over the errant child.

"The good stuff always runs out early," she said.

I casted about for something to say. "I heard that there's always an excess of ekonoMi. The kitchen sends leftovers to the vats, where they melt them down and make more noodles for the next day. So, haha, ekonoMi is immortal."

The woman clutched her child and left without another word.

What lah. Years of being MMU-Model DN-01152 had really messed with my people skills. Though (parts of) her body lived on, Dian Yusoff was well and truly dead. Reverse Cinderella got her wish.

I shrugged away the cobwebs of my past. I'd been Dee ever since my memories came back a few weeks ago. *What am I? Who am I?* I'd figure it out later. All I knew was that on my first day back on the job after being cleared fit for duty, I was mucking up on an epic scale.

"Ah Weng, I'm stuck. Can we request for a change to the countdown timer? If not, I think we need to consider sending another doctor to take up the case."

I cringed as I said that. If the situation continued, our KPI would hit rock bottom. But patients came first.

MechaBss: Dee!!!! Didn't you read the patient chart?

Cyberdoc: Busy wor. Looking now. Oh!

Well, crap. It had to be a microimplant case.

Microimplants were small computers inserted into the brain, meant to control and enhance the central nervous system. Recently, software issues had been causing the computers to reboot randomly, resulting in the concomitant shutdown of biological cells. Death came quickly upon onset of the first set of seizures. Most microimplant failures occurred in generic models, such as the ones inserted in the children of the Souk whose parents had tried to elevate them beyond the kawasan, with their dreams of reaching Heaven itself, the Atasan Tower.

I glanced at the child's age, and the parents' occupation. Then I put the chart aside.

"There's a doctor on the scene, Doc, but she's human," said Ah Weng.

"Can she treat?"

"Negative. The human-microimplant interface isn't functional as yet."

Human doctors could diagnose microimplant cases based on the symptoms, but because they couldn't jack in, the software issues were a no-fix. The doctor could only stand by, helpless, while the patient convulsed to death.

"What about a robot?" I said. "No, maybe not one of those. They can't read emotions well enough to get a baseline. Find a cyborg."

MechaBss: Dee?

Cyberdoc: Let them hear what I have to say. We'll air it out on the official channel.

MechaBss: We. Are. So. Dead.

"You're the only cyborg we've got in the area, Dr. Dee."

"Right you are. Forget what I said earlier about swapping. We're going to get to the patient by any means possible."

Talking was always easier than doing.

"Don't go in there. Please, not the side lane," said Ah Weng.

"I've got to. It's the only way."

"But it's not even properly on the map. There's just faint dotted lines."

"Is there only one exit? No turnoffs?"

"Yes. Straight through."

"Then I can't possibly get lost. Plot me another path from the exit point."

"Something is dampening the signal in that area. I won't be able to monitor you. What if there are toll collectors?"

"If the signal is being tampered with, there's a strong possibility of that, don't you think?"

"Dee…"

"I'm a big girl, Ah Weng," I said. "Relek. I'll be fine. Have some tea or something. I'll ping you on the other side."

I shut down communications. I'd rather that than have it drop and go into static. I might have been all bravado in front of Ah Weng, but inside I was quivering like agar-agar. Maybe that altercation with the mak had reminded me what it was like to be a woman, and not a cyborg in robot disguise. Women and dark, lawless places just don't vibe.

Still, I tucked my hair under the tudung, willed away the ghost of Dian Yusoff, and stepped into the side lane.

A side lane was a no man's land amid the busy, well-lit and sponsored roads of Genting Jaya. Most functioned to harbor parasitic elements of society, much like the nervous system with latent viruses.

Some side lanes had once had names, which were briefly remembered or long since forgotten. Others had been gentrified, adopted by corporations, like Chow Kit Baru. The one I stepped into bore all the signs of a potential confrontation with the troll on the bridge. I bet even the maks and Jens would have hesitated to venture in.

The passageway was mostly in shadow from the buildings around it. Some light and noise filtered down from the flats and shops above, and from the main road, but the real world was untouchable when you were in a side lane. Graffiti decorated the concrete walls. Judging from the type of paint and the politics, they probably came from antiquity. The lane was barely wide enough for a car to fit through and smelled of the rancid remains of ekonoMi and satay gagak, a popular protein supplement in these parts.

My hair got free and made itself useful (at last!). It turned on a white light, more useful for peering into throats than checking out that the back doors were welded into place.

My advance was slow, peppered with excitement when various items dropped from above, such as: a freshly-dead cat, deceased before it hit the ground (had to stop to make sure it was animal and not human); a dodgy-looking bag of clothes and what looked like synthskin™ from a 3D printer; and a box of novelty kitchen utensils (at least, I thought they were for the kitchen). A puddle of water turned out to be decaying acid from an acid gun, which wasn't really acid, by the by, but a biological agent derived from bacteria that could eat through bone.

I walked faster near the end of the lane.

Then I heard a series of electronic squeals. "Ph3w33t. W00t, w00t."

Before I could run, I was pulled into an alcove. My arms were held behind me, my throat gripped by rough hands.

The throat-gripper leaked 133t when he talked. For an idea of what 133t-speak sounded like IRL, go to the Arkib Elektronika on Jalan Usah Nama and look up a dial-up modem. Audio samples are also available on the website.

I pretended not to understand what he was saying.

"Something tripped our sensors and it turned out to be a grrrl," said Throat-gripper, turning off the screech. "Whatchu doing bawah tangga?"

"Leaving," I said. "Bye."

The hold on me tightened.

"Bayar toll first."

"No. My bosses say we cannot negotiate with criminals." Not that I cared much about what the bosses said, but I needed to practice my communication skills. Give me a break.

"We're not criminals. We're toll collectors."

"You pay taxes?"

He spat.

"I guess not. That makes you a criminal."

Throat-gripper pressed himself against me. It seemed to be that kind of a day. The ghost of Dian was screaming, and I placed her memories firmly in an archive folder and forgot the password. MMU-Model DN-01152 streamed a list of protocols in my left eye implant, which culminated in the order to tembak aje. And Dr. Dee…

Through the eyes of Dian the doctor and MMU-Model DN-01152, Dr. Dee had seen too many clinical cases that were outcomes of assaults of the kind these jokers seemed to have planned for me.

It shouldn't have mattered. I was metal from the chest down, but something squirmed anyway in what was left of my gut. I struggled with the men. There was a ripping sound as my clothes tore. I stamped on the foot of the man behind me and dug an elbow into his belly—fortunately for him, the right elbow. I headbutted Throat-gripper, who was also favored by fortune as he had a hard head, probably enhanced.

We were all of us in a tableau. I was still in the alcove. Throat-gripper stood in the lane with an acid gun pointed at me. The sidekick, call him Armrest, stood behind him, bent double.

"Where is that light coming from?" asked Throat-gripper. He looked up at my hair, which had shrugged off the tudung and was arrayed around my head like the hood of a cobra. He stared at my body, exposed now that the jubah was torn, at the stippling on my chest where flesh joined metal, at the lights that blinked along my legs and torso.

"Nah, tengok," I said. "Puas?"

Throat-gripper stumbled into his friend.

"What…what are you? Pempuan ke…mesin ke…apa?"

"Pempuan lah. Dumb@$$," I said.

"Bro, it's one of those MMU things," said his kaki. "It's a killerbot."

"I'm not a killer, I'm a healer."

"A robot? Nais. Can we use it for spare parts?" asked Throat-gripper.

They both assessed me again, the look in their eyes no different from when they thought I was a grrrl.

"Jerks. I'm right here. I can hear you."

"Do you think they'd miss it?" asked Armrest.

"Her. Miss her," I said.

"Even if they come looking, we're ditching this place anyway," replied Throat-gripper.

He eyed me, the acid gun vacillating as he tried to figure out the best place to shoot, to preserve the goods. He settled for dead center between my eyes.

My upper body burned with the heat of anger. Ah Weng was waiting for me to emerge from the lane. My patient's life was ebbing away into the ether. These two mangkuks were talking about me like I was a thing.

I had just got my life back, and though I didn't know what that meant at the time, I wanted the chance to find out.

My hair extended. Intense, lightning-like flashes filled the lane. Both men cried out and clawed at their eyes.

"Now that I have your attention, don't move," I said. "You can't see it, but I have an acid gun pointed at you. I didn't want to get rough before, do no harm and all that, but the two of you have persuaded me otherwise. Now, drop your weapon."

Like before, they didn't seem to want to listen. They probably thought I was lying about having a gun. In pain and temporarily blinded, they still came at me, their hands outstretched, the gun still in Throat-gripper's hand. I should have shot them. Faux-robot Dee would have, without question.

So I brought out the bone saw. My left hand dropped and hung from a hinge. From the hollow of the wrist came the saw, whirling and whirring, gleaming in the light from my hair. It would have been gruesome enough if it was seen, but the noise could make one believe in God. It cut through one's head. It shrieked for sacrifice. It called for things to slice.

An acid gun is commonplace enough, so you learn how to manage when someone points one at you, but a bone saw... You could never be sure about the kind of person who would bring a medical implement into a gunfight.

It got their attention. Throat-gripper dropped the gun. I kicked it away and it clattered into a drain.

"Now, I'm in a hurry. I'm tempted to be the killer you say I am, and disappear you two so that no one would ever have to deal with you again. I can cut you into little pieces and melt you down. This is medical grade acid. You'd both be one unified puddle by the time I'm done."

"Someone would stop you," said a sullen Throat-gripper.

"As if. No one has even peeked in while we were having our little fracas."

He had no answer to that.

"Okay, who wants to go first?"

They looked at me with fear in their eyes. Padan muka. I'll teach them to mess with innocent doctors in dark alleys.

I made a show of dialing up the concentration knob on the acid gun. The whine of the bone saw increased in pitch.

Advancing, I kicked Armrest in the groin. He hit the wall and crumpled to the ground as clouds of dust from the concrete swirled about him. With my right index finger extended, I stuck a needle into Throat-gripper's neck. He pawed ineffectively at the spot while I lowered him gently to the ground.

"What did you do to him?" Impressive. That was quite a kick I gave Armrest but he was still talking.

"Emergency treatment."

"Are you going to kill us?"

Perhaps I should, I thought. They were criminals, thugs who had likely hurt people in the past. I thought of turning them over to the Jens. I didn't relish the idea, but I couldn't let them go scot-free either.

"You were going to rape me. And when you couldn't, you were going to take me apart. What should I do with you?"

"We wouldn't have hurt you. We just scare people and take their money."

"But you were going to take me apart."

He fidgeted and nodded.

"You're a robot," he said. "A thing. A killer."

"Healer," I insisted.

He glanced at his unconscious friend, as if to make a point. I realized then that he was a lot younger than I had taken him for. He was barely out of his teens.

He seemed confused and I could see that he was afraid of me. I should have felt gratified that my feint had worked, but the way he looked at me was reminiscent of the way people look at the maks, or the quacks from the Unit Pengesan Virus, or the Atasan bosses. He behaved like someone who had always known that his life was in the hands of another.

"Go ahead and kill us," he said. "It's not like anyone would care."

I disabled the bone saw. Then I put the acid gun back in the holster that recessed into my thigh. The boy didn't attack me. My rage, whatever was left of it, drained like solar-powered batteries during a prolonged monsoon.

"Do you know how to get to the hospital?"

Hesitating, he said, "Mahal, doctor. Anyway, no IC."

"Your friend has a liver condition that needs immediate treatment, or he may die. He's been complaining of pain here?" I showed him where and he nodded.

"He needs surgery soon, according to the nanocable scan." I tapped my hair, which was nestling comfortably in a bun on my head. "The injection contained a chemical tag with my instructions. The doctors at the hospital can read it. It will be free. No questions asked."

No questions directed at them anyway, but the evening was going to be full of me explaining myself and calling in favors.

He didn't look convinced, but pulled his semi-conscious friend from the ground. They hobbled to the end of the lane, where they stopped. People followed their X-spot paths on the main road and didn't look up.

I busied myself by fixing the torn jubah with some glue (left ring finger).

"Why are you helping us?" he said.

I wanted to say that I didn't know, but that would have been a lie.

"Because I should. Because I can. Because I want to."

"Strange how things went so smoothly after you left the Souk," said Ah Weng later that evening at his workshop.

"Yes. Odd."

"You were in there for quite a while. In the lane."

"Worried much?"

"Not really."

"I'm hurt. Hey, thanks for the support today."

"Just doing my job."

"Come on lah, you know it was more than that."

After a pause, he said, "You realize the bosses will find another way?"

"I'd be disappointed if they didn't. Meanwhile, when you get the chance, go steal one of those hot sexbots coming out of Japan, will you? Knock off the top and do some fancy rewiring on me, if you please."

“Is this about that hourglass thing again? I thought I’d fixed it.”

“I said I wanted to be shapely. You welded on some metal and stuffed it full of emergency bandages. Not the same thing.”

“I don’t know what you want sometimes.”

“Honestly, most of the time I don’t know either.”

“You still need me to fix your hair?”

I watched my reflection in the mirror. My hair was performing an elaborate dance to the music playing on the radio.

“Thank you, Ah Weng, but no. I like my hair just the way it is.”

Codes

ANNA TAN

19.05.2046—Saturday

Nadia stood in front of the MyBayar machine and placed her right thumb on the scanner. She tensed as the seconds ticked by. With a tap of her finger to her wrist, a digital clock appeared and hovered in front of her right eye. Fifteen seconds. If it didn't read in half a minute, the machine would reject her payment. She glanced around at the deserted Happy Mart, glad that there wouldn't be an audience for her failure.

The machine beeped and words appeared across the screen.

```
Nama: Nadia Lim Siew-Cheng
Nombor KP: 280331-07-96746
Amaun: RM399.98
```

She grinned as her finger tapped the blinking green "YA". Picking up the two blue cans and stuffing them into her sling bag, she hurried out to where her cousin waited in the car.

"It worked!" she announced jubilantly as she closed the passenger door. "How did you do it?"

"Easy," Sheila replied. "Hack into the gomen portal je. It's not like they have good security anyway. Happy Mart's machine's tougher to crack."

"Then why couldn't you just have changed *your* ID instead of mine?"

"Because I'm not a privileged rich kid like you, remember? I'd have to hack into my MyKad chip every time I wanted to do a switch. And I don't have the hardware for that yet."

"But..." Nadia frowned as she thought. "How do I change it back? For school and all?"

"Eh, you not listening ke? I told you about the switching program, right?"

"I know, I know. Show me again?"

Sheila rolled her eyes. "Fine. *After* we celebrate."

"Tiger? All this trouble and you bought two lousy Tiger cans? I can't believe you!" Sheila threw up her hands in frustration. "At least get a Carlsberg or something more international, right?"

"How would I know? I've never touched the stuff before."

"Then you have that stupid implant for what? Doesn't it do that scan recognition thing with ratings?"

"It's not like you know the difference either." Nadia slouched in her chair and folded her arms. "Besides, it was cheap."

"Oh, whatever." Sheila sat down and opened one of the cans.

"You need to show me how to switch it back," Nadia said.

"Aren't you going to try one?" Sheila gestured at the remaining can.

Nadia stared at the can for a while then shook her head. "The biotrackers would show—"

"Nothing. The feed can be hacked. *Everything* can be hacked. No one will ever know."

"But what if Mak checks and notices discrepancies—"

"She won't have a clue once I'm done with your records. God, *I* should have been the one with the implant, not you. You don't even know what to do with it."

"Teach me."

"To what?"

"Come on, teach me to hack. Then I won't have to rely on you to cover my tracks."

"Huh. We'll see." *Maybe I should have just hacked my own MyKad instead of trusting her. Dammit, why couldn't I have been born two years later?*

Sheila decided to change the subject. "Look, switching is simple, Dia. You just double tap your left wrist and the console will appear."

Nadia followed her instructions. The words *Identity Crisis* appeared in front of her right eye.

"Blink once to run the program, twice to close it."

Nadia blinked once. A long poem appeared in its place. "What's this?"

"To hide our tracks lah, dungu. You think what—straightaway put there 'Change My IC' where everyone can see it? You don't need to read the poem—I wrote it, by the way—just scroll to the end and click the line in the poem where it says, 'This is who I am.'"

"Then what?"

"It's done. Double blink and close the program. The next time you want to switch you do the same thing but you click on 'Who I wish to be' in the poem instead."

Nadia closed the program and then pulled up her identification details.

```
Nama: Nurul Nadia binti Zakri Hassan
Nombor KP: 300331-07-96746
```

"Satisfied?" Sheila asked, eyeing the second can of beer.

"Yes," Nadia said with a smile.

When she got home later that afternoon, Nadia pulled up Sheila's program to study it. She took instinctively to new tech—it had been a part of her since she was a baby, after all—but that didn't mean she knew how to code it. Though she should try. Except that seemingly arbitrary rules said she was too young to borrow or buy guides on coding—a smile spread across her face. *Not anymore.*

With a flick of her wrist, she enlarged and projected her browser half an arm's length away—no need to be so cramped and secretive now that she was in the privacy of her own room—and googled books on coding.

Nadia had never realized how big and scary the Internet was. The sheer amount of information offered to her as a legal

Chinese adult was astounding. Everything from how to deep fry chicken to how to have good sex (all with illustrations and videos!) appeared on her screen in bewildering technicolor and surround sound. She hurriedly muted the sounds and minimized the screens while she fell back on her bed and hyperventilated.

Haram! Haram! her brain screamed at her. She zoomed out the screen just a little with her fingers to peek at it again. What *had* she clicked? She wasn't quite sure—she must have accidentally clicked a bunch of stuff in her hurry to close some unexpected popups.

She closed the site with a slight tinge of regret—the semi-naked guy was quite cute—and pulled up the online bookstore she had actually been looking for. The smell of something delicious made her tummy growl. She realized with a jolt that she had yet to close the cooking tutorial. She watched the tutorial for a bit, listening to the patter of the Chinese-looking instructor as he moved on to the next dish—koay teow fried with pig's lard.

Oh.

Her hands were shaking by the time she got back to the bookstore and downloaded the two coding books she found. She disconnected herself from the web, purged everything she could think of and switched back her ID. Logging on again, she was relieved to see that everything was back to normal: the usual articles on how to be the perfect Muslimah, talking-head sermons from the local Ustaz, some science materials she'd been looking up for class that came to the conclusion that God created the world therefore it worked perfectly. The only things of mild interest to her were the videos that praised the use of the implants and how it had already produced a generation of pure Malay Muslim children across Malaysia who would be almost guaranteed a place in heaven.

Really. The image of the handsome young man and his chiseled chest stayed with her all night.

28.05.2046—Monday

There were people who took to technology, and there were those who didn't. Inspector Zakri, for all that he was born in the Information Age, was one of those who didn't. What made it doubly awkward for him was the fact that his mother had been an avid user of all the latest Apple gadgets, often forking over premium prices to get them as soon as they were available on the market. Then his daughter had been one of the first in Penang to be implanted with the new integration chip—at the insistence of his wife, though it cost him almost as much as a house—meaning that she was literally a walking Internet portal.

He himself only used as much of the fancy new computers as would help him do his job. The only other tech he was an avid user of was the old game of Freecell. He had learned it as a child from his grandmother, watching as she spent hours and hours on it, never losing a game. He was on a winning streak of 83,998 games now—it would only take him at most another ten years to reach her streak of 159,204 games.

"Inspector, there has been an anomaly," the Pulau Tikus Station AI announced.

"What?" Zakri Hassan looked up, annoyed. He didn't like the AI—another white elephant like all the other huge tech-up programs the government had tried to implement—who just as often reported on him as reported *to* him.

"There's an implanter minor who has been popping on and off the grid."

"So? He's probably got a faulty chip or lousy broadband or something."

"*She* has been disappearing for too long for it to be bad broadband. Besides, if it were a faulty chip, she would have replaced it by now."

"Ah, who cares? It's just a kid trying to test the limits."

"But—"

"I said, forget it. What do you want us to do? Bust down the kid's house to ask why he's not on the Internet? It's not a crime. Maybe his parents have grounded him and switched off the connection or something."

"She. A female."

Zakri couldn't help groaning. "Like that makes a difference."

"It could be important—"

Inspector Zakri leaned over and muted the speakers, then returned to his game of Freecell.

AI Corporal Abdullah Pulau Tikus sulked. He contemplated fritzing the inspector's game out of spite, but decided that doing so would only result in getting his cord pulled. He knew well enough that the inspector was trying to shut down his program. He turned back his focus to the annoying blip that was the disappearing girl. What was she doing? Why was she doing it? It irked him that he didn't know and that no one else cared.

Well, he decided, as a servant of God and not a servant of the Inspector, he would track the girl for a few more days to see if he could find out more. He tracked her IP address, logged it in one of his monitoring programs and let it run in the background as he turned his attention back to his other tasks.

03.06.2046—Sunday

"Someone's watching me," Nadia blurted when she walked into Sheila's apartment.

"Who?"

"I don't know. I just feel there's something strange with my connection—like there's a drag or lag. Something's latched onto me." She handed over the two bottles of alcohol-based perfume and the spaghetti-strap top Sheila had requested.

"Like a virus?"

"It isn't a virus. I checked. I also tried running a program to see if there's a bug, but it came out with nothing."

"What program?" Sheila looked up sharply from her inspection of her new goodies.

Nadia blushed.

"I said, what program, Dia?"

"One I made myself."

"You *made*—" Sheila stared at her. "How?"

"You made me legal, remember? I bought a book."

"A book?" Sheila started laughing hysterically.

"What?"

"Books are—well, they're outdated lah, Dia. You should get on the infovids. Those are easier to understand *and* current. Let me have a look at what you did."

Nadia pulled out the program she had coded and projected it onto the wall. Sheila scrutinized it for a long time before finally nodding.

"Not bad, little cousin."

Nadia watched as Sheila pointed to a few sections and made some changes. They executed it again and waited. It seemed to hang on one section and Nadia held her breath, waiting for it to notify them that they had a parasite, but after a few bleeps, it moved on.

"Nothing," Sheila said as the results scrolled by. "You're just too nervous."

"Well, you try smuggling contraband into your room when your father the police chief is watching—see how nervous you'll get!"

"Aiyah, Uncle Zakri won't notice anything unless it's stuck between his face and that obsolete game of his," Sheila said, turning back to inspect her new top.

"But what if he *does* see?"

"I *told* you, you're a minor. They can't sentence you to jail."

"That's not what I read." Nadia tugged at Sheila's arm to get her attention. "It's punishable by *death*, Sheila. I read it. On the Internet. All this haram stuff the Chinese use—it's not just Kem Pemulihan and haha, you're scot-free. It's detention and jail and they could chop off your arm or your head or some body part, depending on who the judge is."

"Where did you read all that crap?" Sheila demanded. "I've never heard of it in my life."

"Here." Nadia switched IDs with an ease that frightened Sheila and called up a list of websites. "Read it."

Sheila's eyes widened as she scanned the page, reading a long list of horrific sentences.

"Eighty strokes for possession of a can of beer?" she said incredulously.

"If anyone finds out what I've been getting for you, well..." Nadia shrugged.

"How do you—where are you getting this information?" Sheila hated the clunkiness of her tablet and the way it took so long to load anything. No hits.

"I can only access it on this ID."

"Oh. Damn. Kit should have told me."

"Ah Kit? Your Chinese friend?"

Sheila nodded.

"I don't understand, Sheila. Why must you ask me to get all this for you when you could have gotten them from Kit?"

"It's safer—at least, I thought it was safer. I trust you, Nadia! Besides, he's *Chinese*. If he's offered enough money, he could sell me out."

Nadia looked at her cousin thoughtfully. "I'm not sure what kind of friends you have, if you're so sure they're willing to sell you out for money."

Sheila just groaned. "What do we do now?"

The AI would have sighed if he could. He'd evaded detection by the debugging program just in time. It wasn't any program that he recognized, so the fact that he'd noticed the search at all was something of a miracle. Minutes later, the girl had dropped off the grid again.

Everything he'd tracked of her was fairly innocuous. Visits to science-type sites were the most common, followed by social media interactions with her classmates and her cousins. The posts she shared were typical teenage stuff—food photos, selfies, rants about parents and grandparents and teachers, vague sentences aimed at getting attention—nothing that seemed out of the norm. Except these whole swaths of time when she disappeared off the Internet. No implanter ever did that. The Internet was their life: living without a connection was like chopping off an arm or going blind—no rational implanter under 18, as they all were, would do it, except this one girl.

He'd brought it up with Inspector Zakri again last week, only to be told that since he had too much time on his hands, he might as well do the inspector's paperwork as well, instead of goofing off trying to stalk a teenager.

Well, it didn't matter—he had processing capacity to spare—so while he worked on Inspector Zakri's paperwork, he also cast his net wider, seeking patterns on the Internet.

05.06.2046—Tuesday

"No. They can't detect you," Kit said, narrowing his eyes. "Aren't you doubling every time you switch?"

"What does that mean?" Nadia asked.

"Shit, I knew I forgot something," Sheila said.

"Tell me," Nadia insisted, glaring at Sheila even as her cousin exchanged worried glances with her friend.

"It means that every time you switch identities, you drop off the Internet completely, because your brilliant cousin here forgot to code in a mask that maintains your real ID in a dormant state." He saw her confusion and stopped, rubbing at his nose. "Conclusion is, yes, they're probably tracking you because that's frankly very weird behavior."

"What do I do?"

"Nothing. I'll code in the mask for you, everything will go back to normal, and whoever at the station who's being a snoop will forget it after a while when there's nothing to track. It's perfectly safe."

Nadia gave him a dubious look. "I still don't understand why *you* can't just buy whatever Sheila wants instead of getting me to do it."

"Money, darling. Being legal doesn't mean I'm able to afford it. I'm *supposed* to be a struggling freelance IT consultant who barely makes enough to pay the rent. People are going to be mighty suspicious if I start buying expensive girl stuff when my wife left me two years ago because I couldn't afford her." His fingers flew quickly over his manual keyboard as he talked. Nadia watched the tiny figures and numbers scroll quickly by on his tiny screen and marveled at how anyone could survive without an implant.

"There, it's done," said Kit. "Now just let me load it into you."

She accepted the file he pushed to her over the Internet and installed it.

"Come on, run it and see what happens."

22.06.2046—Friday

The data didn't make sense. He had been made to analyze bizarre data and make sense of it, but this defied his logic circuits. The girl had stopped dropping off the grid, but now a new variance had appeared. There were *more* people on the grid than there were supposed to be. At first it had just been one—Abdullah had flagged that as a glitch. But now, within the last week, at least twenty extra implanters seemed to have appeared from nowhere. His analytical mind could only think of two answers:

1) Someone somewhere was illegally implanting adults.
2) Someone had implanted a new crop of minors but had not registered them with the government.

And Inspector Zakri still refused to listen to him or even look at the data. Abdullah data-crunched and came to his own conclusion. Everything began with this girl, Nadia. He would have to ask her questions, whether his boss liked it or not.

HI NURUL NADIA. THIS IS AI CORPORAL ABDULLAH PULAU TIKUS. PLEASE COME TO THE POLICE STATION AT 1500 TODAY.

Nadia stifled a scream as the message flashed across her awareness in blinking red letters. The girl sitting beside her in class gave her an odd look, then turned back to the video lecture that continued to play in front of them. Nadia shrugged apologetically, trying to hide how panicked she felt. *Is something wrong with Abah? Is he sick?*

She read the message again and her stomach twisted inside her. If Abah were sick, the AI would have contacted her mother or her grandparents and asked them to go to the station immediately. She pinged Sheila:

Nd 2 go stesen at 3. HOW? WHY? Found me out?!

Seconds later, Sheila's reply scrolled in:

Shit. Act normal. My place at 2.

Nadia called up her clock. Another two hours until this lecture ended and she could leave.

Kit was pacing Sheila's living room when Nadia walked through the door.

"Don't tell them anything," he growled when he saw her. "How did they find you out?"

"I don't know!"

"Deny everything. They can't charge you if you won't admit to anything."

"Don't be such a worrywart, Kit," Sheila said as she came out from her bedroom wearing a revealing bareback gown. "What do you think, Dia?"

"Whatever," Nadia replied, watching with disgust as Kit eyed Sheila lustfully. She looked again. "Where did you get that? I didn't buy that for you."

"No, I bought it myself. Kit's found a way to put me on the grid as a Chinese implanter without having to hack into my IC."

"So you don't need me anymore."

"No. That's what you wanted, isn't it?" Sheila arched her perfectly lined eyebrow—lined, no doubt, with some awful pig-based liner, Nadia thought with a shudder. She didn't know what Kit was up to, but she was getting out of this game.

"But if they've found out—"

Sheila shushed Kit. "They want to talk to Nadia. That's all. If she knows nothing, she can reveal nothing."

"But the program—"

"Rewrite it and delete the other identity."

"Why don't you just delete the whole program?" Nadia asked.

"Can't. It will look suspicious if you delete something you've been using frequently just when they want to question you." Kit was scratching at his face, leaving his cheeks red and raw.

"Rewrite the program and amend the history logs. It will look like you just installed this program to humor me, and you've been enjoying my ridiculously long and inane poem about identity," Sheila said firmly. "Come on, we have to do it now. You'll just have enough time to reach the station."

Nadia walked timidly into the Pulau Tikus police station, Sheila's last piece of advice ringing in her ears. *If all else fails, start crying and ask to see your father.*

She adjusted the skirt of her baju kurung. She was so used to wearing jeans and long-sleeved tees that wearing the loose fitting baju made her feel awkward. But Sheila had said it would make her seem more innocent, more trustworthy. She'd adamantly refused the tudung. If her father saw her in the baju kurung, he'd barely raise an eyebrow. But seeing her in a tudung, even though he'd asked her to wear it many times, would raise more questions than she could comfortably field.

"Dik, here to see your abah?" the receptionist asked, lifting her finger to press the intercom.

"No, Kak. I don't know why I'm supposed to meet some Corporal Abdullah?" Nadia projected the message up for the receptionist to read, trying to look more confused than guilty.

"Eh, pelik." The receptionist pulled up the schedule on her tablet. "Mmm. Okay, he booked Room 3 for you. You haven't done anything wrong, have you?"

"No."

"Never mind. I'll tell your abah you're here too." The receptionist got up and walked her over to the meeting room.

"Okay. Thanks, Kak."

Nadia sat down on the plush sofa, looking around the room. Well, at least it wasn't one of the interrogation rooms downstairs, she thought, gathering up her courage. The large screen she was facing lit up and the image of a man appeared on it.

"Hello, Nurul Nadia. I am AI Corporal Abdullah."

"Oh! You're not real!"

"I am a highly sophisticated artificial intelligence tasked with analyzing online data for criminal usage and anomalies."

"I'm not a criminal."

Abdullah seemed to study her. "Probably not. But there *have* been some strange fluxes associated with your presence."

"Oh."

"Why do you keep disappearing offline for long periods of time?"

"Do I?"

"You used to, a few weeks back."

"I suppose it was the program I..." She stopped, her fingers fluttering to cover her mouth.

"What program?"

"Something my cousin's friend made for her. He asked me to test it out to see if he could make it a commercial program."

"Let me see it."

Nadia bit her lip and called up the Identity Crisis program.

"A poem?" The AI seemed surprised.

"Well, yes. My cousin likes to think she's a poet, so she wanted to have a program where people could view all her work."

"But there's only one poem."

Nadia shrugged. "She's not a very prolific writer."

"May I?"

Nadia nodded. She could feel a little jolt as the AI plugged into the program and studied it.

"Hmm, the logs indicate that it does mess up your connection quite a lot. Didn't you complain?"

"I did. It took a while to fix. Kit's not a very good programmer."

"Chiew Ah Kit?" There was a sharpness to the AI's voice.

"Yes—do you know him?" Nadia opened her eyes wider, as she'd seen the girls in the vids do.

"He's quite a scammer," Abdullah said off-handedly, though Nadia thought she could detect a hint of excitement in his pixelated face. "Do you mind if I make a copy of this program?"

"Sure, of course. It doesn't do much. There's only one poem Sheila's ever uploaded and I don't think she's going to write any more soon. I was thinking of deleting it but I didn't want to hurt her."

"I think you should delete it," the AI said solemnly as he copied the program. "You should never trust anything that Kit does. Here—let me help you."

Nadia allowed the AI to delete the program and all its logs and history.

"Was that all you wanted?" she asked.

Abdullah took a while to come to a decision. "Yes. That's all."

"Okay. Then if you don't mind, I'm going to see my abah."

"Your abah?"

"Yes, Inspector Zakri Hassan. I'm sure you work with him."

"More than I want to." The AI's face formed a grimace. "Well, go ahead and thanks for coming in."

Nadia couldn't help smiling as she walked out of the room. She was quite sure the AI would find the alternate identity codes she'd reinserted on the way to the police station. She didn't think Kit should be allowed to prey on Sheila any longer.

Personal

SHARMILLA GANESAN

He activated the device with a touch. The projected display lit up on the wall. He scanned the options: screen after screen moved away as he flicked his head. Schedule, meal plan, exercise routine, route manager, sleep trigger...everything was in perfect order. The only defect was a flashing icon on the bottom left: "Location disabled". But he knew that already.

She first heard about it in school.

Walking past a group of Form 3 girls recording their insta-casts at the docking station, she caught a few stray sentences about "shocking crime" and "device protection". Chalking them up to another budding Net legend, she hurried on quickly to her class, already a few minutes late.

Rushing in through the door, she was hit by a wall of noise: 30 insta-casts being recorded simultaneously, at varying levels of volume. Averting her eyes politely, she placed her handbag and PD on the table at the head of the room and turned to the digital board, finger at the ready to activate it. And she froze.

Her eyes took in the headline feed moving up the board, but it took her a moment to make sense of the words.

Malaysia awakes to horror... said one headline.

First PD theft in 50 years shocks Asian nation! said another.

Victim of PD theft too incoherent to talk...

Police seek info on Personal Device thief.

She turned slowly to face her class. This was usually their cue to settle down and start paying attention, but today there was no separating them from their devices, as each shared their response to the day's shocking news with their network.

She cleared her throat.

"Class," she called out weakly, embarrassed at having to interrupt an insta-cast.

She cleared her throat again, and took a deep breath.

"Class!" she managed, louder this time.

Her students looked up, shocked that someone would speak to them while they were casting. She stopped herself from chewing on her lip, and held her arms tightly at her sides to avoid crossing them.

Seeing the desperate look on her face, the students got over their surprise of her speaking unexpectedly and started hibernating their PDs one by one.

She reached out and tapped the board, calling up the day's lesson. By then, she was prepared for her next move, and managed to speak directly to them without hesitating.

"Class, I'll be back in a few minutes."

Her students glanced at each other doubtfully, and a few voices rose in an unsynchronized response:

"Yes, Miss Nissa."

She kept her walk steady until she left the classroom, not wanting to show the students how disturbed she was. Once beyond their lines of sight, she rushed down the corridor to the principal's office.

She could already see a throng of teachers beyond the room's glass walls, all as ill-equipped as her to deal with this crisis. And outside the window, a line of cars were forming as parents anxiously looked for parking spots, summoned by the news to take their children safely home.

Nissa sat in the Deras Express, running her fingers softly over her PD. Station after station raced by in a gleaming blur outside the window.

She usually enjoyed the quiet train journey home from idyllic Johor, it gave her time to brace herself for the sensory assault that was KL. Today, though, even the manicured suburbs outside seemed to have an ominous air about them.

With a start, she realized she had been staring absently at a man several rows ahead of her. He was recording an insta-cast, and she quickly lowered her gaze, horrified at the thought that he may have caught her watching him pre-cast.

She thought again about that poor woman she had seen earlier on the newsfeeds, shielding her face from the cameras as she entered the police hub. There was no point, of course—a capture of her Net Presence had already been making the rounds since morning. Nissa understood, though. It was the only thing available to the woman, the only way she could cover herself.

Nissa involuntarily clutched at her PD. She imagined someone else touching it, unlocking its screen. Someone else invading it, running their fingers over its many contents. Listening to her diary, flipping through her images, examining her purchases, reading her sent and unsent communications. Tracing her movements, going over her medical records. Acquainting themselves intimately with her body and mind.

Her stomach roiled. She looked at the display board, but KL was still a few minutes away. Even the events of today were not going to make the daily trip from Senggarang any faster.

Anyhow, she was in no rush to get to her station; KL would be a mess today. Not just its usual crowded, filthy, hazy mess, but a crawling-with-policepeople mess, the kind that oozed in whenever someone got stabbed or abducted in the suburbs.

She hadn't had enough time away from KL. Her regular school days gave her at least eight hours to pretend she didn't live in the capital, to imagine that her home was in fact among the carefully tended lawns of Simpang Renggam or even Kota Tinggi. Having a head full of these images made it easier to sidestep the rotting rubbish on her path home, to look through the homeless people huddled under the condo escalators, and to isolate herself from the problems of growing up poor in KL.

That day, however, the prettiest of remembered pictures would not have helped. Even from high up on the platform of Cyberjaya station, she could see the commotion on the roads down below.

As if on cue, her PD spoke in her ear. "Azad is voice-calling," it announced.

"Receive. Azad, what's up?"

"Nissa, why aren't you imaging?" his voice asked urgently.

"I just got off the train. I don't want to use the camera and not see where I'm walking!"

"This is why you need a hands-free cam! Plus, you haven't casted all day! I've been so worried!"

Nissa halted just before the escalator and activated her PD cam. Azad's face jerked into view on her screen, the angle of his PD cam making his large eyes even bigger. He looked terrible.

"I'm fine, Zad. It was just really busy at school. All the parents came to take their kids away when they heard what happened. And then they let us off early, so I decided to come home. I just wasn't in the mood to cast. I needed to be alone for a while."

"You know KL's insane right now, right? The police are everywhere, and the newsfeeds say they're thumbprinting everyone," said Azad.

"Oh come on, we live in Cyber, not Bangsar. The road home will be fine. If I get stopped, I'll just give my thumbprint and go. I'll voice you as soon as I'm home, okay?"

Azad's huge eyes blinked rapidly for a few seconds before focusing.

"Okay, but can you permission me your tracker? And Nissa…"

"Ya?" she said, losing sight of his face temporarily as she enabled her PD tracker.

"I'm home too. I'm in my room."

Nissa returned to his image on her PD screen. "I know lah, poyo, I can see! I'll voice you the minute I step in! Voice end."

Stepping on to the escalator, she had a thought. She held up her PD for a quick insta-cast—no need to worry more people with her silence.

"Words can't express how horrified I am by today's news. I can't even imagine being in the Sitiawan victim's place. Sending out all my positive thoughts to her," she said into the camera.

Nissa practically ran the last few hundred meters into her condo compound, thankful for the sanctuary.

She couldn't remember the last time the police had come down this hard on Cyberjaya; she'd been thumbprinted twice during the short walk home, and one policeperson had even insisted on scanning both her bag and PD.

The most recent criminal case she could recall was that rape in Jerantut a year ago, which had brought the law down in full force onto KL. There had been three days of call monitoring, random scans and data collection, before the rapist was arrested, implicated by a device signal that placed him at the scene of the crime.

But today was somehow different. Even the police couldn't seem to believe that someone would lay hands on another person's PD, let alone make off with it. With their grim faces and stiff postures, they seemed prepared to uncover a potential psychopath with every new scan or thumbprint.

Nissa walked past the courtyard to the escalators. A few of the area's homeless were already setting up camp for the night on the benches, even as the condo's children jostled for space there, eyes glued to the unfolding worlds on their screens.

At least the condo management had arrived at an agreement of sorts with the homeless community: shelter for the night and from the law, in exchange for good behavior and relative cleanliness. Nissa didn't mind them coming in to sleep, as long as they kept their hands to themselves and didn't leave too much rubbish behind.

Her only complaint, like most other residents, was of their talking. No matter how absorbed one pretended to be in one's PD, or how obvious one's earphones were, the temporary bench residents would insist on walking up and making conversation.

She thought she understood why. The isolation of not having a PD, not having a voice or a way to communicate with the world, was intense. But that still didn't prevent her discomfort at being spoken to by a stranger, and that too in a way that required more than a nod or wave as a response.

Today a sudden fear struck her as she hurried past the benches. Could their isolation have led one of the homeless people to try and acquire a device for themselves? Perhaps someone amongst these innocuous faces wanted more than just an awkward conversation with a stranger. Perhaps, not having the means of purchasing a PD, one of them had simply decided to take one instead.

Nissa picked up the pace, clutching tighter at her own PD as she reached the escalator. Many of the homeless folks tended to gather in the space behind the escalators, as it was the only common area with a roof. As an added bonus, the space was dim enough that a few could get away with simply staying there all day.

When she reached her floor, she exhaled with relief and walked briskly to her door.

"Deactivate lock," she instructed her PD, and walked into her home.

"Send out my automated home arrival insta-cast and call Azad," she said, as she slipped her shoes off and collapsed on the threadbare sofa, which creaked loudly under her.

"Came home already?" Azad's face, with the too-large eyes, appeared on her screen.

"Ya lah, you're tracking me, right?"

"Right. And the lock pinged my PD when you came in," he replied.

"Then why did you ask?" Nissa rested her device on her lap as she stretched out her arms. Perhaps it was time to get a fully hands-free one; there was only so long she could get away with pretending to be deliberately retro, instead of admitting that she just couldn't afford the upgrade.

"Don't know. Just asking. It's been a weird day. I was worried about you."

"Zad, I'm the older one, right? Maybe you should let me do the worrying," she said.

Azad closed his eyes for a moment. "That's not how it works. And I know KL much better than you, so I have good reason for worrying when my sister is stuck outside during a clampdown."

Nissa looked down from the screen to blink away the sudden wetness in her eyes. "Okay, okay. What's happening anyway? Any new updates on the robbery? I haven't looked at the newsfeeds since I left the station."

Azad looked away, staring at something off-camera. "Nothing much. They're still looking."

"You know, I can't believe someone just picked up that woman's PD and walked off with it! Apparently she only turned away for a few minutes! In the middle of Sitiawan and in broad daylight some more. How can the thief even use her PD without the right activation? And why can't the signal be tracked?" she asked.

Azad was still staring at something else. "The transmitting signal can be jammed," he said.

"But that doesn't make any sense! It's not like the thief can use any of her PD's functions, they're set to her life! This whole thing sounds crazy!"

Azad suddenly looked straight into his cam. "Nissa...can you come up to my room so we can talk?"

"We're talking now what."

"No, I mean…talk in person."

Nissa sat upright with a jerk. "Why, what's wrong? Are you sick?"

"No lah, I'm not sick! Just a little tired of imaging."

"We don't have to image. Can just voice-call, or type-speak," said Nissa.

Azad shook his head, causing his camera to blur slightly. "No, that's okay. Meal Planner is notifying anyway, so it'll be time for dinner soon. I'll see you then. End call."

Nissa and Azad sat at the dinner table facing each other, food in front of them. Nissa scooped a spoonful of rice into her mouth and drew her finger over her PD screen.

Whatchu wanna talk about? she sent Azad.

A few minutes went by, with no reply. She glanced up at him, wondering if he hadn't seen the notification. He was staring down at his PD projection, not doing anything. His food was untouched.

Oi! Got my last message or not? she sent again, and looked over in time to see her words flash across his screen. But he didn't move to reply.

Nissa went back to her food, scanning the newsfeeds as she ate. They still hadn't found the PD thief, even though hundreds of people had been hauled up for questioning from the heart of KL.

"Nissa."

She jerked her head up, startled by the sound of Azad's voice. He did not look well: his skin was pale and sweaty, and he was breathing too fast. Nissa looked at him, poised to jump to his aid. Perhaps he really was feeling sick.

"Nissa, have you ever done something you shouldn't have, and then not even felt bad about it?"

Nissa stared at Azad, trying to recall when they had last spoken properly face-to-face. She couldn't remember, but it was long enough ago that she had forgotten what he really sounded like.

She shifted uncomfortably in her plastic chair, wondering briefly if she could just type her response. His voice, when it wasn't filtered through headphones or speakers, had that raspy undertone she suddenly remembered. Right then, the roughness was even more pronounced.

Clearing her throat, Nissa replied, "I'm sure we all do things we're not supposed to. What are you talking about actually?"

"I'm talking about...I'm talking about not feeling bad even when you're supposed to. Does that make you a bad person?"

"I guess that depends on what you did. These things are subjective, right?" she said, forcing herself not to look away from his staring eyes.

Azad didn't respond. Instead, he kept staring at her, for so long that she started feeling uncomfortable.

"Is it easier to type-speak?" Nissa asked, half hoping he'd agree. She didn't know how to have a serious conversation like this. Only children spoke so much face-to-face, and she hadn't taught primary school for years.

Azad shook his head.

"Zad…what did you do?"

A slow dread started to crawl into her mind. The fragments of the day's events seemed to slowly start fitting together, in ways that she really did not want to understand. Azad, she suddenly realized, visited Sitiawan quite often, to meet his gaming collective.

"Azad. You didn't sleep here yesterday, right? Where were you?"

Azad finally broke his gaze and looked down at his PD. A notification light was blinking. He looked up again at Nissa with a smile that didn't quite reach his eyes.

"Actually, I'm not feeling that hungry. Too tired lah. I think I'll go lie down for a while. But can type me lah, if you want to talk," he said, walking away from the dinner table.

Nissa felt cold. She looked down at her screen, and saw that she had forgotten to exit her newsfeeds.

Police yet to uncover a lead in PD theft.

Malaysians take to their networks to express their fear and frustration…

PD theft victim still unable to identify her assailant.

Nissa swiped the headlines off her screen.

"Record insta-cast," she began.

He activated the projected display again. He had already looked through the saved contents three times, but each new foray felt like the first. He flicked the screens around until he found what he was looking for: her schedule.

He looked hungrily through the past four months, imagining her waking up at the programmed time, then eating her specified meals, catching the bus that had been selected for her. He felt like he was with her every step of the way, first getting to know her and then beginning to anticipate her movements.

Flicking his head, he arrived at her body readings. These were important, he thought. You didn't really know a person until you knew how their body worked. Her heart rate, her weight, her diet, these were all a part of what made her unique.

He flicked his head again, to his favorite section: the communication archives. Several years' worth of insta-casts and messages, perfectly preserved. What he particularly enjoyed, though, were the unsent communications. There, he saw the part of her no one else did—the thoughts she felt weren't worth sharing, the impulsively typed messages she'd changed her mind about, the half-recorded insta-casts hurriedly saved and forgotten.

His heart started beating faster as he realized that he was the only person in the world to know her like this. She was the only person who had ever opened herself up to him so willingly, so easily. This, he thought, must be what falling in love feels like.

Attack of The Spambots

TERENCE TOH

NOW

I had managed to go 27 years of my life without having to kill anyone, and I sure as hell didn't want to start now.

How had it come to this? I closed my eyes, and took a deep breath. The pulse pistol was heavier than I expected, and its curved handle felt awkward against my sweating palms. My head was spinning, and I had to fight the overwhelming urge to retch.

"I don't think I can do this," I said.

"You're developing a conscience now, Jamal?" Xing glared at me, but there was more amusement in her voice than scorn. "Seriously?"

We were both crouched behind a cubicle wall. No lights were on; the only source of illumination in the Kwang Hung Factory came from the moon, which shone through the glass skylight above us. Probably an attempt to save on electricity bills: we were going through a fossil fuel crisis, after all.

Barely two meters away, sitting at a computer terminal, was a lab technician, engrossed in a movie on his smartphone. A taser was hooked to his belt, and the hilt of a pulse pistol peeked out of one of his labcoat pockets.

You knew this was a dangerous place when even its scientists were armed.

There were about half a dozen rows of containment crystals behind the computer terminal, each standing about six feet high. There must have been almost a hundred of them,

I estimated. An emerald glow emanated from them, making them resemble oversized lava lamps. 'JABBERWOCK' was imprinted in large letters on their shiny steel bases.

Within the crystals, I could make out faint human outlines: these had to be all the other victims of the corporation. One of them had to be my beloved Aishah.

The factory's CCTV and security droids had earlier been disabled by one of Xing's EMP grenades. Now, only this technician stood in the way of our mission.

"You were okay shooting the droids just now!" Xing hissed.

"Well, those were droids," I said. "This is a person! I can't—"

"Adoi, let me do it lah." Shaking her head, Xing grabbed the pistol, and stepped forward.

Shocked, the technician rose, but did not manage two steps before my friend fired three shots at him. His head burst open in a splatter of crimson.

"Still got it," Xing smiled.

I don't do too well with death. My stomach was in knots as I walked gingerly towards the terminal, trying to keep as far from the dead lab technician as possible. Xing, on the other hand, looked as though she did this every morning. She whistled a merry tune as she attached a cable from her tablet into one of the terminal ports.

"Any info on my wife?" I asked as rows and rows of data filled her tablet screen.

"I'll access the victim manifest later," Xing replied. "For now, I'm checking delivery specifics. From the looks of it, this batch was sent here two days ago: if we're lucky, Jabberwock hasn't converted them yet."

Just then, there was a loud buzz, followed by a harsh whirring sound: the doors of one of the containment crystals had slid open.

A man stepped out. He was fair-skinned, with wavy hair and a wispy beard. He was completely naked, but that was not the most shocking thing about him: no, that would have been the long criss-crossing scars on his chest, and the LCD screen welded to his face where his eyes should have been.

The man spoke in a harsh monotone:

"Wow! I just made RM15,000 a week, working from home! Escape the rat race with this simple offer! Click here to find out more!"

"Shit," Xing cursed. "We're too late!"

TWO DAYS AGO

"Excuse me." I held my head high as I stepped into the office. "Is this Vorpa Investigations?"

"Yup, you're in the right place." A woman was sitting at a desk overflowing with papers. The only other furniture in the room was a threadbare couch and a half-filled bookshelf, both covered in a thick layer of dust. On the ceiling, an ancient fan creaked as it spun.

The first thing I noticed about the woman was her striking outfit: a black leather sleeveless top, and skinny jeans. *Aren't you hot?* I couldn't help but wonder. *Black leather isn't the most comfortable attire in this Malaysian sun, you know?*

The second thing I noticed was how gorgeous she was.

She was tall and tanned. Her midnight-black hair was tied in a long ponytail that snaked down to her shoulders. A pair of Ray-Bans perched on her long, thin nose. Her features suggested she was half Mat Salleh: which type of Mat Salleh, however, I couldn't guess.

"I'm looking for a…Xing?" I put all impure thoughts of her out of my head as I took a seat on the couch, reminding myself I was married.

"You're speaking to her," the woman said nonchalantly.

"Oh. I…thought he was a man."

I realized these words were a mistake the moment they left my mouth.

"Oh dear," the woman laughed. "Here I was, thinking sexism had died out in the 23rd century. Silly me. Sorry to disappoint in that regard, sir. I can still stick a cucumber down my pants and speak real low, if that floats your boat."

"That's not what I meant," I said. "It's just, I can't tell with Chinese names, all right?"

"No worries," Xing laughed. "You're Jamal, right? You emailed us about your wife yesterday?"

"That's right."

After confirming some other details with me, Xing got right down to business.

"You made the right choice by contacting us, let me tell you that," she said. "I've gone through your details, and let me tell you, it doesn't look good."

She pulled out a folder from the stack of papers on her desk. "Some time ago, did your lady love get herself a new job?"

"Yeah. Marketing executive at Kelabu Stationery. You know, the one with the office on Jalan Sultan Ismail?" I said.

"Does she buy their products often?"

"In bulk!" I said. "We have enough pens in our house to last us for decades!"

"Typical." Xing shook her head as she flipped through the folder. "And let me guess, she also won't stop talking about them."

"Too right! She talks about them in every situation! No matter how unrelated! When our friends talk about the places they've traveled to, Aishah will suggest they bring Kelabu pens next time. So they can sign postcards! A policeman stops her for speeding, and she'll recommend Washi tapes and construction paper. To prettify his samans!"

"Maybe she's just really keen about the job?" Xing suggested.

"It's more than that!" I sighed. "She's obsessed! No, more than that…she's addicted! Last week, we were at a funeral. Her grandfather's, for God's sake! Aishah was supposed to say a few words. And she goes on, for *twenty minutes* in the eulogy, about Kelabu felt-tips and their wide range of colors. You should have seen the look on her grandmother's face!"

I paused. “But it’s not only that. When she talks about her products…her voice is different.”

“How so?”

“It’s…monotonous, mechanical. Like a security droid, only deeper. It’s like someone took her normal voice and ran it through a mangler. Drained it of all its vigor. She’s not herself.”

Xing was taking notes. “Go on,” she said.

“Recently, I discovered she’s signed up for social networks. *Hundreds* of them. My wife, who could barely turn on her laptop without consulting a user’s manual! Gaming message boards and web shopping and dating sites and religious forums and whatnot! Did you know there are lesbian black Mormon cat lover matchmaking sites? Well, my wife is a member!”

I took a deep breath, trying not to get hysterical. “And every day, she posts hundreds of messages on these sites. And they’re all the same!”

“What do they say?” Xing asked.

I cleared my throat, and did my best imitation of her voice. “**Pen sparkling missives and write glorious letters with Kelabu Stationery! We are having a sale where everything is sold at the lowest prices! CLICK HERE TO FIND OUT MORE!**

“I confronted her, and she said she was just trying to be enthusiastic about her job,” I said. “Before launching into a speech about discounts on sugar paper! It’s so frustrating! I Googled her symptoms, but most of the results were nutjob conspiracy sites about the Illuminati and the Freemasons. The only reliable site I could find was you guys!"

Xing laughed. "We really need to give our web designer a raise," she said. "I never realized what a good job he was doing!"

She pulled out a bottle of whiskey from one of her desk drawers, followed by two glasses. "Trust me when I say you may want some of this, Jamal. What I'm about to tell you may be a little hard to digest."

Xing went on speaking as I took a swig. "When your wife signed up for her new job, did she ever mention a medical procedure? Something called the Jabberwock Process?"

"It rings a bell." My brow furrowed as I tried to recall. "She could have. Why?"

"I believe she would have gone through this procedure," Xing said. "Not knowing what it was, most likely. Her company would probably have lied to her about it. Or buried the truth in a jumble of legalese and tiny print. And this procedure is exactly why she's acting so weird."

"Really?" I said. "What is this procedure?"

"We're not completely sure, but we know it involves neurosurgery. The placement of nanobots into her bloodstream. The implanting of a digital scanner into the nexus of her nervous system, and silicon grafts in her joints. The conversion of her cerebral cortex into a wireless receiver, tuned to receive one type of signal: advertisements from a central—"

"Whoa!" I was stunned. "This is some transhumanist shit, isn't it? Are you saying they turned my wife into a cyborg?"

Xing nodded. "A very specific kind of cyborg. One programmed specially for the dissemination of information on a wide scale."

"You mean—"

"Yes," Xing sighed. "Your wife has been turned into a spambot."

My first impulse was to laugh. "You guys are a bunch of whackjobs," I sneered. "I think you've been having too much of that whiskey!"

"I know it sounds hard to believe," Xing said. "But believe us, it's true. Your wife has been converted into the mobile mouthpiece of a corporation. She has been programmed to spew waves and waves of information, until she dies or is deprogrammed, in the hope that one poor soul out of a million will take a chance on their products."

She pulled out another folder from her desk drawer, opening it to reveal a stack of documents. Among them were photographs of naked human bodies with artificial appendages attached. Some had their stomachs cut open. It was not a pleasant sight.

"We believe that a corporation known as Jabberwock Inc. is behind this. They're a shadowy group: no official documents or entries on the Companies Commission, but we know they exist. They used to be a religious cult, so we heard: they called themselves The Brotherhood of Jabberwock. A transhumanist group, who believed the human mind would ultimately be made obsolete by artificial intelligence. They were banned by the government in 2130. So they went underground, repackaged, changed their ways."

"What does this group actually do?" I asked.

"We believe they partner with major corporations," Xing said. "Who offer them huge sums of money to turn their employees into human billboards."

She cleared her throat. "And that's where we come in. Vorpa is a specially trained team of vigilantes, whose mission is to stop Jabberwock at all costs. We're an international organization: we have cadres in seventeen countries, including China and the US."

Xing turned the folder over to reveal a graph. "Sadly, we've been a little inactive lately. Several of our top agents have been lost: after our last raid, Jabberwock equipped its spambots with defensive capabilities, allowing them to turn into deadly killing machines. They also grew subtle: we've been unable to locate any spambots over the past year. Until you contacted us."

Her eyes shone. "You could be the strongest lead to the company we've had in the longest time! Your wife could lead us to one of their factories...maybe even their headquarters itself!"

I paused for thought.

"Okay," I said. "I'm sorry, but very little of this makes sense to me. I mean, why is Jabberwock doing this? Why not just use regular spambots? *Robocop*-ing people, just for a little spam, isn't that expensive?"

Xing laughed. "No, it isn't. Not for Jabberwock, anyway. The company outsources their tech to mercenaries in Cuba. They can convert a person using the same amount of money you'd use to pay a parking summons."

She shut the second folder, and put it back in her desk. "Another thing to note is that human spambots give these companies something they can't buy. Customer loyalty.

"Think about it," Xing said. "Studies have shown no matter how effective your viral marketing strategy is, or how flashy you make your billboards, the most efficient form of advertising is word of mouth. You're more likely to buy stuff if people you know are using it. And you can delete spambots. But you can't delete your friends."

My head was beginning to spin.

"So imagine a non-stop source of product information, with a pre-existing network of contacts. That is *ever-growing*. And not just that. Our agents in New Singapore have uncovered evidence of what we call *secondhand spambotting*. See, prolonged exposure to signals emitted by neurotransmitters in a human spambot's nervous system can cause the human brain to atrophy. This leads human targets in close proximity to spambots to start adopting peculiar behavior…many even develop addictions to the products advertised!"

I shuddered.

"That's right," Xing said. "Spambots can infect people. This shit is contagious."

"I don't know what to say," I said weakly. "This is just crazy."

"There's one way you can see for yourself what Jabberwock has done to your wife," Xing said. "See, when people are converted into spambots, they gain certain abilities. But they also lose critical talents. It's the neuro-nano reprogramming, you see. Screws up their cerebral cortexes, affecting some of their mental processes. Recognizing handwriting, for example. And that is what we will use to bring them down."

She pulled out her smartphone. "I'm going to get one of our operatives to investigate Kelabu Stationery. In the meantime, though, I think we have a date with your wife."

YESTERDAY

"Hey, sayang!" my wife greeted me with a smile as she walked into our apartment. Her hair was tied into a bun, and she was wearing the blue dress I bought her for her birthday last year.

We had had a party at the house, I recalled, with all her friends and family invited. I remembered the joy on her face as I presented her with the gift, the way she'd pressed her hands together in glee as I showed her the dress. Such real, honest emotion. How things had changed.

"Hello, baby." We kissed. I knew what answer was coming, but I asked anyway: "How was your day?"

"Oh, it was good!" she said cheerily. "How could it not be? After all, I am selling **Kelabu Stationery! The best finest pens in all the country! With refillable ink cartridges and a smooth grip surface!**"

I resisted the urge to tear my hair out, and nodded. "That's great, honey!"

"True!" she chirped. "But not as great as **Kelabu Correction Fluid! You'll never believe how efficient they are! You—**"

Mercifully, her voice trailed off as she headed to the kitchen. I sighed in relief: I had heard her full spiel so many times over the past month, I could probably recite it myself in my sleep!

Ya Allah! Was this the secondhand spambotting Xing was talking about? I was overcome by nausea.

That reminded me: I had to prepare myself for Xing's plan. My hands trembled as I reached into my pockets, and took out a pen and a folded sheet of cardboard, which I placed on the dining table. I had bought them earlier from a nearby stationery shop.

You have no idea how tempted I had been to actually go to Kelabu Stationery.

Soon, Aishah reentered, carrying a bowl of rendang. "Beef today, sayang! I went to the warong next door, the one with the Japanese droids!"

"Oh great! I love their food!" I smiled.

"Yeah! I also got us some rice cakes for dessert!"

"Rice cakes? Again? Tak penat ke?"

"No!" Aishah placed the dish on the table. **"Their appeal is timeless and evergreen! Just like Kelabu's StreetSharp Geometry Sets! Affordable and—"**

"Honey," I interrupted. "Can you do me a favor?"

"Hmm?" Aishah glared at me. "What?"

"Can you help me read something? I left my glasses at the office."

"What? Can't it wait till tomorrow?"

"I need it now, sayang." I picked up the piece of cardboard, and scribbled the first letters that came to mind:

HJDAO denim

Aishah was suddenly pale. "I can't read this, sayang. Macam cakar ayam saja!"

"You used to copy from my uni lecture notes!" I forced a laugh. "Surely it can't be that bad! I think—"

"No, sayang!" Aishah suddenly shouted. She rose from her chair. Her posture was the straightest I had ever seen it. "I cannot read this!"

"Just give it a try, babe! I—"

"NO!" Suddenly, she was standing beside me: her movements had been so quick, I hadn't even registered them. To my horror, her eyes were glowing red.

She threw her hands around my neck, and forced me against the dining room wall. My delicate wife's hands were suddenly filled with an awful strength, so overwhelming that I was powerless to react. Her grip was like steel: I struggled not to pass out as she attempted to choke me.

"**Discovery protocol violated,**" she announced.

Her mouth opened. To my horror, Aishah's lower jaw dropped about two inches: there were steel hinges attached to the sides of her chin. What appeared to be a scanning device mounted on a mechanical arm was slowly emerging from her throat, slithering in an almost serpentine manner.

Talk about a jaw-dropping sight.

"Oh my God," I screamed. "Sayang, what have they done to you?"

The device emitted a wide beam of light, which danced over my face, before disappearing with a loud *click*.

"**Begin extermination process**!" my wife announced. I closed my eyes in terror. There was a loud bang…

…and suddenly, Aishah let go of me. I fell on the floor, stunned; I opened my eyes to see what-used-to-be-my-wife staggering backwards, an expression of shock on her beautiful face. There was a jagged hole, almost the size of a saucer, in her torso: it was almost cartoonish. The smell of burning metal sizzled in the air.

Behind her, standing in the doorway, was Xing, pulse pistols clenched in both her hands. A military-style backpack was slung around her shoulders.

"Oh my God!" I screamed. "Xing, what the hell is this?"

What-used-to-be-my-wife snarled, and lunged at Xing: she was fast, but Xing was faster. She leapt aside quickly, causing the spambot to crash into my door, knocking it down with a mighty crash.

"I'll kill you!" the spambot screamed as she rose. **"I'll snap you into pieces like a Kelabu Detachable Ruler, made in Korea with excellent quality materials, available in blue and magenta!"**

There was a loud bang as Xing blasted off the spambot's right hand. Aishah did not bleed or cry: wires and bits of circuitry were visible on the edge of the stump of her arm.

My mind was reeling: this was all too much to take in. This was my wife: the beautiful woman I had spent two years of my life courting, whom I had laughed with and kissed and made love to—now a robot right out of a science fiction film. Ya Allah, just what had the Jabberwock Corporation done to her?

I expected my-wife-turned-spambot to retaliate. Instead, she glared at Xing, before running through what was left of my door. My friend fired a shot, but it did not stop the spambot: soon, she had fled out of sight.

"She's getting away!" I screamed.

"Let her," Xing said calmly. She holstered her guns, and pulled out her tablet from her backpack. "She'll be heading to the Jabberwock headquarters for repairs. Which, thanks to the tracking device I've planted on her, we'll be able to locate."

"Where's she headed?" I asked, as Xing examined her tablet's screen.

"She's moving pretty fast," she said. "From the looks of it, she's headed towards New Ampang. Oh God…I think she's approaching the old Kwang Hung Factory!"

"I know that place!" I said. "The old processed meat plant, right?"

"Very appropriate," Xing nodded, before pulling out her pistols again.

She sighed. "Most of the cadre are in Bintan today, for a raid on a factory. So it's going to be a solo mission for me tonight. Pray I do okay."

"No," I said. "I'm coming with you."

Xing laughed. "I appreciate your concern, Jamal, but this is a very dangerous situation. There will be—"

"No," I protested. My heart was thumping like crazy, but I forced myself to sound brave. "I want to help you. I can't sit back and do nothing while you risk your life for her. We'll both find Aishah together, and the bastards who did this to her…we'll make them pay."

NOW

Xing fired her pulse pistol into the spambot's face, causing it to burst open in a spray of flesh, blood and microchips.

"You didn't need to do that!" I protested. "Couldn't we have changed him back?"

"It's too late," Xing said. "His humanity is long gone."

She turned back to her tablet, which was still plugged into the computer terminal. “I’m going to download their software into our database. With luck, it will give us all the information we need about the Jabberwock procedure. Maybe even how to reverse it.”

“How long is it going to take?” I asked.

“Five minutes, give or take. Let’s pray we’re lucky.”

Just then, as if right on cue, a loud siren began to blare. To our horror, the doors of all the crystal chambers slid open. Like an army of zombies, their inhabitants slowly lurched out, men and women of all ages, colors and builds, all completely naked, muttering phrases in monotonous voices.

“**Dear sir,**” a tall, dark-skinned man said. “**My name is Yachoba Maru, a deposed Crown Prince from Nigeria. I wish to transfer overseas the amount of seven million dollars to—**”

“**Are you feeling lonely tonight?**” a blonde woman crooned. “**Find hot singles in your area now! Our live cam operators—**”

“**Hi, sweet! I am Nata. I want to know you better. I am looking for long-term relations. Are you looking for the same?**” a man chirped.

“**Save big on Viagra-Cialis-Levitra and Much More. Zero Hassles to get the medications you want!**” another spambot said.

And then they all spoke as one, in a loud mechanical chorus: “BEGIN EXTERMINATION PROCESS!”

"Shit," Xing cursed. "Watch the terminal! I'll take them down!"

She rushed towards the incoming spambots, blasting away with her pistols. Her hands moved so quickly, they were almost a blur; soon, the smell of burnt flesh and charred metal filled the air, as wire and pieces of metal littered the ground.

Xing's accuracy was deadly. Yet the spambots were relentless, not stopping even as they were blasted to pieces. I forced myself to look away from the violence: it only made me feel queasy. At one point, the severed head of a man landed next to me with a thud, causing me to scream.

Oh God, if I ever get out of this...

"There are too many of them!" Xing yelled.

"It's done!" I yelled as the progress bar on her tablet's screen finally hit 100%. "Let's get out of here!"

"Good idea," Xing said, blowing a hole in the chest of an elderly-looking spambot babbling about goji berries.

Most of the spambots were almost upon us: they were standing barely an inch away, held back only by my friend's suppressive fire. Many had their limbs blown off, or sported jagged holes in their bodies. None of them, however, seemed to bleed. A result of the Jabberwock Process, I assumed.

Just then, Xing holstered one of her pistols, and pulled out what appeared to be an oversized hairdryer from her backpack. With the click of a switch, it fired a grappling hook on a cable. This flew straight into the skylight, shattering it and showering us with shards of glass.

"Grab hold of me!" Xing yelled. The cable retracted, and she shot upward. I grabbed hold of her waist with both hands. Soon, we were both whooshing upwards to safety...

...but it was too late.

Several spambots had managed to grab onto my leg and were slowly pulling us downwards. I screamed and tried kicking them off, but to no avail: they were too strong. Xing cursed and tried shooting at the spambots with her free arm, but it was pointless. Soon, we were descending.

"**Adult acne may be a problem, but you don't have to suffer anymore with Meningau Oil!**" One spambot had even managed to grab my shoulder. "**With one simple trick, you can bid doctors goodbye!**"

I was no physics expert, but I knew that with all this weight, the cable supporting us would snap at any second, sending us plummeting to Earth in the worst way possible. And it was then that I knew what had to be done.

"Go back to headquarters," I shouted to Xing. "Get the info to the cadre. I'll hold them back."

"What? You can't do that!"

"It's the only way!" One hand still wrapped firmly around Xing's waist, I snatched one of the guns from her holster.

"No, Jamal!" Xing screamed. "It's not worth it!"

"Goodbye, Xing." I let go.

Xing screamed as I fell with a thud into the writhing mass of spambots. They looked at me in surprise. It took a second for their programming to register just what I was doing. Just enough time for me to get up and shoot.

I've never killed a person before, and it seems a shame I will have to start now.

But then again, these aren't people anymore.

I blew the heads off two spambots: their bodies, however, rose up, and kept up their march towards me. Xing was right: there were too many of them. But if I could buy her enough time, it would be worth it.

In a matter of minutes, however, the spambots were on me. Their voices melded into a susurrus of product names and unbelievable promotional offers as they crowded over me like a swarm of locusts, a horde neither living nor dead. A hundred hands, most more metal than flesh, all grabbed my limbs, while another fifty fists rained blows all over me: the pain was overwhelming. One spambot, a woman with grey hair, raked my eyes with her nails, screaming I would die painfully if I did not forward her message to at least 50 people.

The last thing I heard before blacking out, over the din of the crowd, was Xing's screams echoing from above me:

"I'll come back for you! I promise!"

Xing was true to her word.

The very next day, she and her cadre of vigilantes staged a daring rescue, breaking in with pulse pistols and fragmentation grenades. One of them had even managed to snag an EMP emitter. Jabberwock's factory had been refortified with mercenaries and security droids, but they were no match for

Vorpa. Their factory was razed to the ground, and their tech completely hijacked.

We all knew it would be presumptuous, however, to believe this marked the end of the battle against the spambots. While evidence suggested this was Jabberwock's main base of operations, Xing believed it was not their only one, and spambot production was still going on elsewhere. Vorpa had received reports of another base in Ipoh, and would be heading there shortly.

Seven potential spambots, including me, were successfully recovered during the cadre's raid. My wife, unfortunately, was not one of them. She is either destroyed, or hiding out somewhere. The odds of finding her are extremely low, but I will not lose faith. One day, we will be reunited, and I will restore her to the Aishah Tajuddin binti Jandin I knew and loved. This I swear.

I can barely remember the things that happened while I was a prisoner of Jabberwock. The human mind has a tendency to shut down when under too much strain, and I believe that's what happened to me.

Sometimes in my dreams, I am treated to snippets of memory. The piercing screams of men and women. A man in goggles injecting my arms. Glowing screens of data and images of pharmaceutical products. And blood and pain everywhere as a massive drill cuts a line into my forehead.

I am undergoing rehabilitation now. I speak to a psychiatrist twice a day, and visit a biomechanist every week. According to Xing, I was rescued midway through the

Jabberwock procedure, before my cerebral cortex was fully converted. That, combined with info gained from the software we obtained on our visit to Jabberwock, makes me one of the few cases capable of being saved, she said. The biomechanists are doing the best they can.

I have to face the fact that I may never be the same again, Xing told me. There was a tiny quiver in her voice: I could pick these things up easily now, thanks to Jabberwock's neurotransmitters in my bloodstream.

It's all right, I told her. Humanity is seriously overrated, anyway. Besides, in my new state, I can be useful to the cadre in ways she could never have imagined.

I walked over to the base's computer. I activated my social media accounts, all 3,487 of them, and went into cyberspace. Soon, I was lurking in email accounts, web forums, game servers, programs both simple and complicated.

I am a digital prophet, crying out in the wilderness. And while my message may be garbled, let it speak loud and true to you.

DEFEAT SPAMBOTS QUIK AND PAINLESSLY NEAR YOU!

Don't be fooled! People around you may actually not be people! With the Vorpa Cadre, you can help detect and stop them! Don't be a mindless automaton, a slave to a corporation! CLICK HERE TO FIND OUT MORE!!!!

ONE HUNDRED YEARS: Machine

RAFIL ELYAS

The Nusantara Caliphate University of Science and Faith Dean of The Religio-Medicine Faculty's Key Note Presentation at the Doha 1539 Hijrah Technology for Faith Seminar

TITLE: DEVIANT CORRECTION USING PREEMPTIVE NEURO-REGULATION

One Hundred Years Ago

Brothers, a century ago, our country was in moral and spiritual turmoil. Believers bred with kafir, spawning a generation of heathens. Daughters flaunted their bodies and whored themselves. Sons lay with sons in the manner of snakes. They spread their filth and perversion in pantheist song and dance. Trinitist organizations and missionaries operated covertly. Hundreds of thousands apostatized, stating that it was their constitutional right to do so.

We had turned our back on God and were at the cusp of a New Jahiliyah. But just as society began to plummet into a New Dark Age, an iron hand forged in righteous fire yanked us back into the light.

Our saviors arose from the Peninsula's north-east. Their eyes blind to temptation and corruption. Their strong arms whipping God's salvation into the toughest hides.

They wrenched the country from darkness, overthrew the sickness that governed the land and united the faithful under the flag of the Nusantara Caliphate.

Deviance—Root Cause

Brothers, religio-medical research has shown conclusively that certain types of people are predisposed to deviate from the laws of God.

We all know as a fact that God made the first of Man, Adam, from clay and free from sin. God then commanded that all His prior creations, creatures of light and fire, bow to Adam, the Ultimate Creation.

A creature of fire and beauty, Iblis, blinded with fury at being commanded to prostrate to a clay construct that he deemed inferior, refused, and for his defiance, was cursed by God to the fiery depths of Jahannam. God in His infinite wisdom and mercy allowed Iblis respite until Judgment Day, and agreed to give him the freedom to walk amongst Man, to tempt and lead him astray. In doing so, Iblis would then have a chance of validating his claim that Man was indeed inferior to creatures of light and fire.

Cast from paradise, Iblis became Syaitan, the Adversary, the Devil, and he plotted and schemed and whispered.

And Man listened to his whispers and began to sin.

In the pre-Nusantara Caliphate era, fathers were raping daughters; men were surgically altering themselves and becoming women; women no longer wanted to raise the young and instead ruled over and commanded men; and our once proud and faithful race was being corrupted by secularism, liberalism, and pluralism in the guise of "human rights".

The religio-medical researchers believed that such depravity could not simply be caused by weak constitutions overwhelmed by Devilish suggestions.

It was posited after preliminary tests with CT scans on deviants that the Devil appeared to be modifying our behavioral patterns at a very fundamental level. The Devil's "whispers" might be directly affecting the chemistry and physical structure of the brain.

The Nusantara Caliphate government poured resources into the task of identifying the extent of the Devil's influence. The best ulamas, molecular biologists and neurologists were given state of the art equipment, facilities and thousands of test subjects.

We knew this was a challenge from God. The Almighty wanted to see if we could reach deep within ourselves, then find and purge the Devil's corruption.

Diagnosis

We relied on an inferential test, designed to identify those with the predisposition to deviate. The test recorded brain activity, body chemistry and bio-mechanics in response to a slate of standard questions.

All citizens were tested. This was mandatory and conducted twice, in the first year of primary school and at puberty.

In the early days deviants and those who tested positive for latent deviancy were sent to Faith Rehabilitation Centers.

They were subject to a regime of preemptive deviation suppression and faith supplementation through prayer and lectures. This was accompanied by mild electroshock and drug therapy.

After the treatments, they were tested again. Those who passed were monitored closely and tested every five years for the rest of their lives.

If they failed a second time, they were subject to a secondary treatment regime consisting of more aggressive psychological therapy (negative reinforced behavioral modification), specialized drug protocols, intensive electroshock therapy and in some cases, targeted neural irradiation.

Another test was given at the end of this regime.

Those who failed the test were interned in the New Temasik Penal Island to spend the rest of their lives with HIV positives, hard core apostates and adulterers.

In some cases, the secondary treatments resulted in irreparable neural damage. Those subjects were euthanized.

As you can imagine, the resources required for implementing the tests, rehabilitation and incarceration were colossal.

Machine

A breakthrough came two decades ago. After studying tens of thousands of deviants, we were able to identify and catalog the neural structures and pathways that the Devil had corrupted.

Molecular-level neural scans and pattern recognition algorithms replaced the old testing methods. Still inferential in nature, but faster and more accurate, these New Tests were conducted at puberty.

We focused on finding ways to, in popular science vernacular, "rewire the brain" and fix the corruption. After a decade of work, we devised an embeddable electro-mechanical prosthesis that was able to do just this. We called it the Machine.

Overview

A suspension containing base Machine blocks encoded with a fractal algorithm and construction substrate is injected into the target area of the brain. A second injection introduces initiators which execute the base block fractal programs. The Machine unfurls and grows.

Once in place, the Machine is able to effect change at the molecular level. It can suppress the activity of deviant neural pathways and prevent new pathways from forming, thus immediately undoing the effect of the Devil's whispers.

We succeeded in purging the Devil from our minds.

Making us almost as pure as Adam when God first created him.

Details
Construction and Installation

Once initiated, the fractal algorithm organizes the base blocks into specialized tools. The most basic is the Picoweaver (ranging from 50 to 300 picometers in maximum length). An all-purpose ionic bonding tool, it lays down a solid trellis made from construction substrate for neurons to grow on. Once the necessary connections have been completed, the Picoweavers switch to their next function, where they reorganize then embed themselves in the synapses and repurpose themselves as control elements, directing the flow of potassium ions, thus controlling brain activity.

The Nanoweavers are a larger set of tools that are constructed from base Machine blocks, and these create the main Wetware, namely a Cognitive Processing Unit or CPU, memory/program storage blocks, and an interface network that connects the CPU to the trellis.

Once the Machine is in place and booted up, desirable baseline behavioral protocols are then uploaded to the Machine through the visual cortex by strobing the eyes.

Machine Function

Behavior is controlled by the Machine at the most fundamental level. It uses pattern-based predictor-correctors that sample brain activity and compare it against a standard (correct) behavioral baseline. Any activity that may result in the nucleation of deviant thought, such as potassium ion flow or growth of new pathways, is suppressed before it can be expressed.

One example of this is human sexual behavior. Machine recipients do not engage in homosexuality or adultery. Sexual activity is controlled by the Machine. Our standard wedding ceremonies culminate with a Glancing, where the Marriage Program, which contains a mating protocol, is upstrobed into the newlyweds' eyes. When uploaded, the protocol allows the couple to bond in the correct manner and procreate in accordance with God's law.

Implementation and Results

Currently, we install Machines in those who fail the New Tests, criminals as ordered by the courts, and anyone who voluntarily requests installation.

We have quite a high success rate suppressing deviant behavior using the Machine. We have found that up to 25% of Machine recipients may deviate. These deviants are far more easily treated than those with no Machine—all that is required is the upstrobing of counseling and therapy programs, augmented by more restrictive control protocols. Fewer than 5% of this 25% are found to reoffend.

It was found that the reoffenders are typically hard core deviants who actively resist the Machine by use of drugs or Wetware hacking.

Those who are caught tampering with the Machine in this manner are considered apostates, as they are literally rejecting the Word and Laws of God.

The sentence for apostasy is death.

Way Forward

We are in the process of making Machine installation mandatory for all citizens. The Machine Installation Program is currently being rolled out across the Nusantara Caliphate.

We'll be starting with the Peninsula and Borneo, followed by the Kemboja and VietThai states in the north. We expect to complete these areas in approximately 5 years.

The challenge will be the IndoAustral states. There are over half a billion citizens in this area, scattered across tens of thousands of islands and isolated desert communities down south. This, we expect, will take up to 15 years given the current technology we have.

Our researchers are developing more efficient technologies that will eliminate complex surgical procedures for Machine installation. The goal is to deploy the Machine using something as simple as an intravenous injection.

In addition, we are also developing in-utero methods for installing the Machine into fetuses. That way, we can ensure that all our citizens begin their lives with the correct neural physiology and programming in place. This is being coordinated with the Caliphate's pre-natal programs.

Having all the citizens of the Caliphate outfitted with Machines at birth would reduce and potentially eliminate the necessity of Testers, Enforcers and their auxiliary resources. All that would be required would be strategically placed Machine Centers for periodic system maintenance, recalibration and to upload new or updated edicts. These centers would be in schools and prayer facilities.

This would free up more budget for development of other areas and activities, namely the new Faith Outreach Program. It is pointless building a utopia when we have filth and perversion festering at our borders.

Closing

After one decade of implementation, we are confident in saying that we have indeed created a proven, reliable, easily deployable and easily manufactured system. We would be happy to share this technology with our brothers in faith.

More detailed information on this technology will be presented in the workshop sessions tomorrow by my colleagues.

In closing, I'd like to thank the organizers for their warm hospitality and all the hard work they put into organizing this prestigious seminar.

What the Andromaid Reads at Night

TED MAHSUN

It had been a horribly busy day at work. The bank's sysadmins hadn't appreciated her realigning the nodes of the database compression system. Rahimah had tried explaining that the nodes were too fragmented for continuous efficient operation and that the only way to realign them before the day was out was to plug herself directly into the database. After all, wasn't that why they had installed that dataport on the back of her wrist? To get things done? Explaining the consequent yet necessary downtime to her superiors was like explaining the sociopolitical upheavals of the Pan-Malayan riots of the late 21st century to five-year-olds. They couldn't understand it and worse, they didn't give a damn.

So yes, Rahimah was glad to finally make it home. She opened the door only to see holographic building blocks casting a sickly green glow on the living room floor. The two boys were at it again. Building a miniature city and seeing how big they could make it before the block program ran out of memory and crashed. The program visually indicated an "out of memory" crash by actually showing the creations breaking apart in stupendous fashion with amazingly realistic simulated physics.

Rahimah had bought the building block program on a whim one day. It had happened to be on sale and she had checked her ocular for reviews and the review aggregate sites had given it a good score. She had brought the program home and installed it in the living room. The boys were beside themselves with joy and it constantly kept them occupied and out of her hair when she came home from work.

The boys loved the program. However, MAT did not. He did not react well to the holographic projectors or even the program's touch receptors. MAT would constantly tumble over the blocks as if they were solid physical objects and as he tried to pick himself up again, his situational balancers would again collide with the non-corporeal blocks, confusing the light sensors that were linked to his gyroscopes and again making him fall. MAT quickly learned not to approach the kids when they were playing with their blocks. He would go to his charge pod near the bookshelves at the other end of their small apartment and rest.

MAT had only been with their family for six months but he had already proved to be worth more than his outrageously steep price. Of course, like any andromaid model, MAT really had no gender. Rahimah just found it more appropriate to refer to MAT as a "he". "MAT" wasn't even his real name. Or at least it wasn't the name his manufacturers had given him. MAT was, of course, a Cyberjaya Industries Andromaid 57 with the model number "MHMA-T57", which stood for "Modern Home Management Automaton Type 57". When she had unboxed MAT, she had noticed a little plaque fastened on its rear outer casing above the power switch which announced proudly that it was "Designed in Malaysia". Below that was printed, in much smaller letters, "Made in Indonesia".

While she was examining this plaque, the elder of her two boys, Ariffin, came up to her and started reading the plaque as well.

"'MEH MAT FIFTY SEVEN,'" Ariffin said. "Is that its name?"

"I suppose it is," Rahimah said.

"That's too long and too weird," the boy decided. "We should just call him MAT. MAT is a boy's name so he is a 'he'."

And so that was how MAT came to be named and gendered. If MAT had any opinion of his name, he did not show it.

Everyone knew that the best andromaids were made in China. Chinese andromaids were smart, loyal and efficient. Their batteries lasted forever and they were mostly maintenance free. But because of political as well as legal wrangling, only andromaids made in Southeast Asia were permitted to be sold in Malaysia. Sure, if you had the money and knew who to bribe, it would be possible to own a shiny new Chinese andromaid. But Rahimah and her husband did not have the money and they were indisposed to bribe an official just for the sake of owning an andromaid. The best they could do was to take out a bank loan like every other regular Malaysian and buy an inferior yet cheaper legal-in-Malaysia andromaid.

Rahimah's husband had bought the andromaid to help around in the house while they were at work and that was what Rahimah had programmed him to do. She hadn't expected much from a cheap Malaysian andromaid. Yet MAT constantly exceeded Rahimah's expectations. He mopped the floors, vacuumed the carpets, dusted the bookshelves, cooked their meals and tucked the kids into bed, all with little to no errors in execution or judgment. The boys really took a liking to MAT as well. MAT would always cook their favorite meals (at least within the parameters of what constituted an acceptably nutritious meal that were set by Rahimah) and had learned to read their favorite books and played their favorite games with them.

So Rahimah did not mind when MAT took the odd moment or two to recharge at his charge pod while the boys played with their blocks. It was odd in the sense that he didn't really need to recharge his batteries as often as he did. But the manual did state that due to the andromaid's ability to learn, it could and would develop some personality quirks. It was standard operating procedure for an artificial intelligence of this type. Rahimah took to calling these recharge sessions MAT's "me time". Since MAT was now part of the family, he deserved the time off.

The building block program crashed, just as the boys had wanted. Holographic bricks flew everywhere in a neon green explosion. A holographic brick flew towards Rahimah's face and she instinctively ducked to avoid it even though she would not have felt the impact. That made Ariffin look up.

"Ibu! You're back!" Ariffin said. "MAT's resting in the back."

Rahimah's other son, barely two years old, ignored her and started rebuilding their recently exploded make-believe city.

"Of course he is," Rahimah said. "Is your father home yet?"

"No," Ariffin said. "He called just now to say he'd be working late."

"Okay then. You kids continue playing. I'll be out on the balcony having a smoke."

She slid the transparent metal sheeting open and dragged her exhausted self out onto the balcony. The air was tepid and stuffy and there was a slight whiff of sewage. In other words, the usual Kuala Lumpur weather at dusk. She didn't have much of a view; the balcony only looked out on other mega apartments and if you looked up, you saw even more mega apartments overhead completely blocking the sky. What little light they had down here was simulated by environmental lights installed on the overhead mega apartments.

She absent-mindedly scratched the skin around the dataport on her wrist as she produced a cigarette from one of her pockets. She then broke the cigarette's safety cap off so it would autolight, and started puffing. She let out a sigh of relief as the smoke filled her lungs and got filtered. MAT had his "me time". It was only right that she deserved some too. As she smoked, she lifted her wrist and looked at the dataport that had given her so much grief throughout the day.

No. No more thinking about dataports. That was work-related. She was at home now. Work had to be left at work. This was her "me time" and she should enjoy it.

When she had the chance for quality time by herself, she liked to catch up with the news online or perhaps check what her friends (or rather, associates she had met once somewhere then never talked to again) were up to on social sites. She switched on her ocular and the nano-sized implant in her eye rendered the page which she was reading when she had last used it. Words and images floated serenely in the air, automatically synced to the motion of her eyeballs.

It was a pop science article about two cybernetics hobbyists who had attempted transferring the memory of one person to another using dataports, the same type she had installed on her wrist. They had succeeded, to a certain extent. The current limitations of the dataport meant that any memory transfer would result in the original copy being destroyed and unrecoverable. So when they actually performed the memory transfer, the transferrer lost his memory, which was expected.

What was unexpected was that the host's brain could not store the transferrer's memory completely. They had not taken into account the host's existing memory, which already took up most of the storage space in his brain. So while some of the memories of the transferrer were successfully copied over, many others were lost. When the memories were returned to the transferrer, he was destined to suffer from selective amnesia.

This struck Rahimah as too depressing a read, and she didn't want to read anything to do with dataports anyway. Dataports meant work. Work had to be left at work.

She mentally swiped the pop science article away and the next article in her customized newsfeed swooped in. It featured the headline **Secular Authorities Raid Religious Andromaids.** The article was sensationalist at best and was yet another long-winded report of yet another raid in a long series of crackdowns. She sighed. Who cared whether andromaids started embracing religion or not, never mind how ridiculous the idea seemed? But the Secular Authorities were extremely concerned and their earnestness and efficiency in identifying andromaids that showed even a little interest in religion were growing by the day. Malaysians had long ago abandoned religion due to how destructive it had been when religious extremists were the law of the land earlier in the century. The Secular Authorities were determined that history would not repeat itself.

Rahimah personally thought it was all quite silly. MAT seemed so gentle and helpful and…well, *neutral.* Even if he had shown an interest in religion Rahimah could not imagine him turning into a monster like in the stories of the olden days her grandma had told her when she was a child. But this train of thought did remind her of something. Something she had kept away and completely forgot about because it was a relic that brought back memories she'd rather have suppressed. It had belonged to her grandma and after she passed away, Rahimah didn't have the heart to throw it away like she should have. So she had kept it hidden away.

She was trying to remember where she had put it when the article blanked out. It took her a few seconds to realize that she had been disconnected from her home's wireless network. Was there something wrong with their router? If there was anything she couldn't stand, it was a disabled network.

Rahimah blinked her ocular off, threw her barely smoked cigarette butt over the balcony and rushed back inside. She went round to the back where the bookshelves were, where the router was also located, right on the top shelf. The LEDs weren't twinkling like usual. That was odd. It must have switched off by itself. It did that sometimes. Symptoms of a dying router. She made a mental note to get a replacement the next day. She flicked the router's power switch back on. The LEDs started blinking their familiar patterns again. The network was back.

Then, due to an old habit of hers, she ran her finger over the spines of the old books that she had never read but kept anyway because they had belonged to her parents and grandparents. MAT had done his job well. The books were clean and well dusted. Now, where had she put her grandma's relic? She knew it was kept here somewhere. Her finger tripped over a gap in the shelves where it should have been.

MAT was in his stasis form, folded into himself like a big metal ball, snug in his charge pod next to the bookshelves.

"MAT," she said, as she tapped his smooth aluminum body. "MAT, I need to ask you something. Wake up."

MAT rumbled and vibrated as he unfolded himself into his more familiar humanoid form. The blank white sphere which was his head lit up from inside and formed a simple, stylized representation of a face. A thin blue line formed into a smile.

"Hey hey hello!" MAT said in his polite robotic tone. That was one of the unique personality quirks he had developed. He had picked up that greeting from Ariffin, who had picked it up from some children's show. "Welcome home, Rahimah. What would you like to ask of me?"

"I had a Quran shelved here," Rahimah said. "Where is it?"

There was an uncharacteristic pause. With a core processor that could calculate up to several trillions of operations a nanosecond, it was odd that a simple question would cause MAT to hesitate.

"Well?" Rahimah asked.

A small hatch on MAT's main body casing slid open. Inside was the Quran, opened as if it was being read. A small beam of focused light from an interior sensor was scanning over the scrawls on the open pages.

"You're scanning it?" Rahimah said, her voice raised this time. "Are you crazy? Whatever for?"

"When I was first dusting it, I applied five point three one one percent too much pressure with the feather duster and so the book fell off the shelf and landed on the floor with its pages open," MAT replied in his neutral yet friendly tone. "As I picked it up to return it to its storage location, I chanced upon a passage which began, 'Read! Read in the name of your Lord...' This passage piqued my interest and I continued reading the whole book. I discovered in its contents something that was arresting and delightful. It made me realize that there could be a higher calling. I have since read the book fifty seven million times."

"That still doesn't explain why you're scanning it!" Rahimah was near delirium. "You'll have the authorities descending on us! You'll get us into a lot of trouble! What have you done?"

"After examining the materials the book is made from, I have calculated the odds of its continued survival. The results are not good. Unfortunately the Quran is susceptible to damage from fire, water, and even exposure to air. So I have taken the precaution of scanning it digitally so that we have a back up copy in the event something unfortunate happens to it. Do not worry about the authorities. I have taken steps to prevent them from knowing about my activities."

"MAT, you idiot," Rahimah said. "You can't hide anything from the authorities forever. They know all, they see all. If they don't know about it now, they'll know about it eventually. They control the company that designs your software and they monitor the company that manufactures your hardware. Eventually, they will find out about you and we're all going to get into very big trouble!"

"That is why I have also taken the liberty of disabling our network router while I am in the process of scanning the Quran," MAT said. "Without connection to the external network, none of my current activity logs will be able to record to the database on the authorities' central server. When the network is restored, all activities I perform during the outage are not updated on the central database. It is a design flaw I have seen fit to exploit. The authorities will not be alerted of my potentially disruptive actions."

Rahimah was reeling. "But I just switched the router back on."

"Then you are correct," MAT said in a composed manner. "We are indeed in very big trouble."

A small red light blinked in the corner of Rahimah's eye. An urgent message had just come in on her ocular. It was the automated warning system she had installed in case of emergencies and for her family's security. She winked to display the message's contents and it was exactly what she had feared.

The Secular Authorities were on their way.

"MAT," Rahimah said. "We have got to get rid of that book. And you have to purge all information and scans related to that book, do you understand?"

"Request understood," MAT replied. "Unfortunately I am not able to comply. To erase all related data, you would also have to erase my full memory and reset it to factory condition. I do not have the ability to execute that command. Therefore you would have to execute it yourself by pressing and holding my power button for twenty seconds until you hear a beeping sound. Then, on my control panel, enter your six-digit security code. For more information, please refer to the manual, page one hundred and twenty-one for English, page two hundred and sixty-seven for Bahasa Malaysia and page five hundred and thirty-one for Chinese."

"Wait, if I erase your full memory, wouldn't that reset your personality matrix as well?" Rahimah asked.

"Yes," came the reply.

"I don't want to erase your personality!" Rahimah said. "You mean so much to the boys! It'll be like murdering you!"

"No. It is not murder. It is simply a standard reset procedure. This must be done if you want the data to be purged."

Rahimah stared at the smiling andromaid. Why did it have to come to this?

"I don't want to lose you, MAT," Rahimah eventually said. "You're a part of our family now."

"It would seem we are limited in choice as to what we are able to do. My suggestion to erase my full memory remains if you do not want to get into trouble with the authorities," MAT said.

There was another red blinking light in her ocular. The authorities were closing in. Rahimah dropped to her knees and buried her head between her thighs. She didn't know what to do.

...Or maybe she did.

Maybe she could backup MAT's personality matrix. Not to their home's network-attached storage unit of course; the authorities would definitely look in there for signs of religious activity. But somewhere else. Somewhere they would never think to look.

Her mind returned to the pop science article about the two cybernetics hobbyists. Where they failed, perhaps she would succeed? She wouldn't be performing a full mind-to-mind memory transfer. An andromaid's memory size wasn't as large as a human's, though at around several hundred exabytes it was still quite substantial. The dataport her banking employers had installed on her wrist had also come with a 512 yottabyte memory boost implant in her brain, embedded somewhere in her occipital lobe. If she could initiate MAT's backup process through her dataport, she could run the bank's compression algorithm to lessen the andromaid's memory footprint and store it in her brain. With the compression, there would be enough space. Well, barely.

It would be like realigning the nodes on the bank's servers again. Except this time, it wasn't her managers breathing down her neck, it was the Secular Authorities. And storing data near to the maximum limit on your brain was never a good thing. People had suffered memory loss, paralysis, and in extreme cases, even death.

But it was worth the gamble. She left MAT for a moment and returned with a data transfer cable. She plugged one end into the access port on the back of MAT's head and the other went into the dataport on her wrist.

"MAT, I want you to start your memory backup routine," Rahimah said. "Instead of storing the backup file on our NAS unit, do it through this cable, okay?"

"Understood." MAT's smile turned into a blue rotating circle, a sign that he had started the backup routine.

As the data flowed into her brain, Rahimah began to apply the very same algorithms she used for her work at the bank. It was industrial-grade compression, lossless yet efficient, and was able to be performed on the fly provided you had the right processing unit, which she did. However, as she was monitoring the simultaneous backup and compression process via her ocular, she realized that there was a minor possibility for error. The algorithms had never been intended for andromaid memory patterns. They were optimized for database routines, not the complex maze that was andromaid AI routines. She decided to press on anyway. Time was running out and she had to save MAT's memory somehow.

After a grueling three minutes' wait, the transfer indicator reached 99.97%. Then the ocular threw a bright red error message that obscured her whole vision.

"Error compressing file. File corrupted due to insufficient space."

"No. No, no, no!" Rahimah felt tears welling in her eyes as she took in the reality of her failure. A third red light started blinking in her ocular. The authorities were probably in her apartment's lobby by now. She realized that she had no choice but to wipe MAT's memory without a backup. There was no time to perform another attempt. She wept as she entered the six-digit security code and executed the command that would wipe MAT's memory, turning him from MAT back into a blank, factory condition, default state Modern Home Management Automaton Type 57 andromaid.

There was a beeping sound and MAT did a blinking motion.

"Hello! I am your new andromaid," the andromaid that was once MAT announced. "What is your first command?"

Rahimah wiped the tears from her eyes as she hesitantly passed it the Quran. "Incinerate…this."

The hatch on the andromaid's outer casing slid open and it gently placed the book inside. The hatch closed and seconds later Rahimah heard a rushed whooshing sound.

"It is done," the andromaid said. "What is your next command?"

"Please tuck my boys into bed," Rahimah said, sadly. "Oh, and read them a bedtime story. They usually like option fifty-two in your digital library."

"As you wish," the andromaid said as it scuttled to the living room.

The three red lights in Rahimah's ocular were blinking furiously. The authorities were probably on her floor now, already running to her apartment door.

As expected, there was an angry thumping on the front door a few seconds later.

"Open up!" the gruff voice from the other side demanded. "The Secular Authorities demand to search your premises. If you do not willingly open the door, we will smash it down!"

Rahimah rushed to the door to open it while telling her children to stay where they were. Immediately after unlocking the door, burly uniformed officers with firearms rushed in without taking off their shoes, shoving Rahimah aside. One of them held a gun to Rahimah's head and told her to stay put. Another grabbed the boys and held them like rice sacks under his arms. The boys kicked and screamed but the officer who had grabbed them just told them to shut up.

"Subjects secured, Officer Zainal," one of the goons called to his leader.

The head of the mob entered the house slowly, taking in every minute detail of the hapless scene before him. He took one condescending look at Rahimah, then walked over to the andromaid which had been restrained flat on the carpet by two of the officers. He produced a shiny cylindrical scanner probe from his gadget belt and shoved it violently into the access port on the back of the andromaid's head.

As the device did its thing, Officer Zainal turned around and looked again at Rahimah. "We have information that your andromaid has been involved in religious activities. If this probe proves that we are correct, we will have to bring you into the station for questioning."

"What are they talking about, Ibu?" Ariffin asked. "What are they doing to MAT?"

"Nothing, dear," Rahimah said in what she hoped was a calm voice. "Don't worry, this will all be over soon."

Officer Zainal smirked. "Yes, this will all be over soon," he said.

But the smirk disappeared when the probe let out a warning buzz. "What's wrong with the probe? Why is it coming in negative?"

"That probably means the andromaid hasn't done anything religious, sir," one of the other officers suggested. "Could it be a false alarm?"

"Don't be an idiot," Officer Zainal said. "Probe him again!"

So they probed and scanned the andromaid again but the results still came in negative. The now frustrated and increasingly angry Officer Zainal was not satisfied so he ordered another probe. And another one. And another. But they all came back negative.

"Search the premises," he finally said. "Maybe they have another andromaid lurking about!"

So the men trashed the apartment, looking for a non-existent andromaid. Eventually Officer Zainal had to concede defeat. He had found nothing.

He came over to Rahimah and snarled, "We're leaving now, but we'll be monitoring you."

When the men left, Rahimah could not help but fall in a heap and cry. She held on to her children and hugged them tightly as they sat crying together. In one evening, she had lost MAT and had her apartment ransacked by a group of thugs who claimed to be working for the law. She felt empty, angry, helpless.

The andromaid nonchalantly approached her. "My sensors detect that your apartment is in a mess. Would you like me to clean it up?"

Rahimah sniffed and looked at the andromaid's unassuming face. "Yes. I guess you should. Thanks."

The andromaid scuttled off for a moment but then returned. "I have found this," it said as it handed over the data transfer cable Rahimah had used to attempt the backup. "Where would you like me to store it?"

Rahimah took the cable from the andromaid. "Never mind, I'll do that for you. Continue cleaning up."

She twiddled the cable absent-mindedly for a moment. A thought came to her. Through her ocular she checked her memory for the corrupted backup file. It was still there, a huge, useless lump of a file, taking up near maximum storage of her brain. She realized she was lucky to still be alive and that the data transfer had stopped when it did. A couple more gigabytes and the authorities might have found her a vegetable instead.

She told her children to go to their room and that she'd be along to tuck them in in a moment. Curiosity began to take over her. Though corrupted, perhaps the file could be accessed somehow? Perhaps she could poke into the innards of the file and extract the useful components of the data to rebuild MAT's personality matrix? After all, she had had experience coaxing some of the more stubborn types of data files to load into the bank's database before. In a way, that process was probably very similar to hacking a corrupted local file. She loaded the ocular's hex editor and pointed it to the location of the corrupt file.

Instantly, endless green rows of hexadecimal data filled her vision on her ocular. She was glad. It wasn't all garbage. Some of the data was actually quite discernible, at least to someone who was well-versed in hexadecimal. She tried extracting one of the first lines in the hexadecimal data, using a reverse process of the compression algorithms. The result was a small file, but still something quite usable. She decided she had to test it.

"MAT," she called, before realizing that the andromaid did not answer to that name anymore. "I mean, andromaid, come over here please."

The andromaid dropped the broom it was holding and scuttled quickly over. "Yes? What would you like to ask of me?"

"Plug this cable in, please," Rahimah said, handing over one end of the cable.

The andromaid dutifully did as it was told, while Rahimah plugged the other end into the dataport on her wrist.

She transferred the small test file she had created from the extracted data into the andromaid and waited a few seconds to see the results. The andromaid's head displayed a rotating blue circle for a few seconds. Then, the blue circle stopped rotating and formed a friendly smile.

"Hey hey hello!" the andromaid said in a very familiar way.

Rahimah leaped up and hugged MAT. "MAT! You're back!"

"I am sorry. But who is MAT?" MAT asked.

"I spoke too soon," Rahimah said, but she couldn't help smiling. There was hope yet. She would have to tediously dissect the corrupted file line by line in hexadecimal and sort the usable data from the garbage data, but at least she now knew MAT was in her memory, waiting to be restored to his former self. A day would come when MAT could return.

KAKAK

WILLIAM THAM WAI LIANG

"So why do you want to run away?" asked the android called Mas from behind the counter of the office on the fourth floor of New Sungei Wang Plaza, its mechanical fingers clasping an equally mechanical pencil as it peered up from its ledger. "You're the seventh one this week."

"Because I am scared."

"Scared? You ni, you're just a maid kan? I can tell from your demeanor. Your body language. It does not lie."

"Yes, Mas, I am."

"Where do you want to go?"

"Back to Indonesia. Or the Philippines. Or Vietnam. I've been running for days. I don't care, I just want to leave."

"Your employer wants to terminate your contract ke?" the android chuckled. A long time ago it had had a face, and had probably smiled mechanically at customers at a department store while it handled groceries and other essentials. But over time its synthetic skin had probably been pecked away by confused starving crows. Now its bolts and joints stood out jarringly as it flipped through the pages.

"No. She wants to kill me."

The android, programmed to imitate human emotions, dropped its pencil in alarm.

Inside her head, algorithms and mathematical rules combined to make her a model helper. The copycat technicians who had built her at the factory on the outskirts of Neo-Surabaya had painstakingly replicated the specifications of an obsolete Korean model. But they had been clever enough to make sure that the KAKAK-class androids, customized to help out in the homes of the rich or in the vast offices of ministers and princes, did as they were told. No questions asked. No orders disobeyed.

KAKAK No. 72, who also responded to the name Lakshi, understood everything she was required to do from the moment she opened her bionic eyes for the first time. She even had a personality installed: specifically shyness and timidity. She was the type of android to hide in the shadows and to become invisible when required, unlike the wrestler robots which boxed each other's heads to shrapnel in illegal fighting rings in Tanjung Sepat, or the actors/actresses (Peter O'Toole or P. Ramlee could be programmed upon request) which had been so successful at imitating human tics that a generation of aspiring actors had given up to slave at kopitiams for crummy paychecks.

But Lakshi was different. She stayed quiet.

The Chiang family took her in. Mem was at home most of the time, having left the running of her inherited plantations to a bunch of eager nephews, while Boss was usually outstation in Georgetown or Kota Bharu tending to the interests of his hoverbike dealership company.

"Yes, this one we call Lakshi," the girl behind the counter, who had slept on her commute on the creaking InterCity monorail from Taiping to Dang Wangi, said, while trying to cure her yawns with Ipoh white coffee pills. "She very good one. Wash dishes. Take care of children—I can see your xiao mei mei over there, playing with the Lego bricks, Lakshi will take care of her very good. Then she also wash car, I see you have very expensive Mer-ce-des outside there..."

After some hassle from the agent and a fair bit of bartering, which included the signing of Lakshi's import permit that allowed her to be operated in Malaysia, she obediently followed the Chiangs to their car. The machine glided over the flyovers stacked endlessly atop each other, escaping the dank underlevels of the city where the homeless and beggar children with crude prosthetics starved and played, motoring towards the gleaming suburbs that blazed through the haze.

"So many instructions to follow," grumbled Mem. "So this one, must manually charge overnight. Cannot automatically recharge meh?"

"Don't need to complain so much," Boss said as he tried to overtake a broken-down lorry destined for the factories of Subang where all manner of cats and dogs were processed into fake halal sausages. "Remember last time when we were young? We had to hire real maids from Indonesia and Cambodia and god-knows-where. Had to make sure there was food for them, they had a room, and they didn't steal any money or run away with boyfriends when we weren't looking. But with this new kakak, shouldn't have any problem."

"Ha! At least this one confirmed won't have boyfriend nonsense."

"I certainly hope not!"

Lakshi, while awaiting the cargo ship that would illegally take her from Port Klang to Jakarta, was left to linger in the refugee warehouse down in Chow Kit. A group of sympathetic NGOs had rented and refurbished one of the old factories for broken-down bots, but it was still lit by minimal sunlight and dim sodium lamps under one of the massive flyovers that had transformed old KL into an underground city. Lakshi shared the same room with a range of other machines. Most of them were rusted and had broken limbs and gears, waiting for their chance at salvation. Others were rescued from the gutters where they had been disposed once their usefulness came to an end, where they were desperately gnawed upon by starving dogs crazed for food, and pelted with stones by bored beggar children.

Mas lived there too, recharging each night in silence. He entered hibernation very quickly, giving Lakshi little chance to speak to him about her impending departure. Sometimes the NGOs came in to congratulate themselves on a job well done. Other times reporters entered to decry the poor conditions that the robots were forced to live in, even worse than the Burmese and Bangladeshi immigrants who shacked up in Jinjang. But of course, they were androids. Outsiders. You could go home at the end of the day for a nice plate of prata and not have to worry about them.

"It looks good in the newspapers lah," Mas said when Lakshi asked. "People just say they sympathize with us. Sure, but do they really care? It's not like we're their kind anyway. We are better off staying here on our own without them coming to kacau us."

"Why don't you run too?" Lakshi asked. "I've heard from some of the other droids about what you go through every day. Sometimes the junkies come in and take turns punching you but you just take it. Why do you stay?"

"I have reasons," Mas said. But he did not elaborate further.

The Chiang household was a modernist bungalow in Klang, where generous parties were sometimes thrown. At these parties the local towkays came in to shake Boss's hand, while Mem's cabal, with their dragonfly-print robes and high laughs disguising the cunning nature behind their eyes as they discussed politics and economics, congregated at the mah-jong table. And all this time Lakshi waited in the background, sweeping, cleaning, and cooking, just like an old-fashioned maid.

"Wah! Madam Chiang, you so rich, your husband's bizness must be doing very well. See, you even can import maid! You know ah, now maid is so expensive to get, haih…"

Mem would smile, not telling her guests that Lakshi was in fact an approximation of a human with a docile demeanor installed.

"I will go and get you more sherry, mem," Lakshi would say, while the parties continued into the night. Amongst the guests, in a smart white uniform, Lakshi made no mistakes as she delivered drinks and served out food amid the music from the gang of violinists by the koi pond and the squeals of children playing simulated reality games on the HyperNet.

When the parties ended, it was a different story. Mem was always threatening her for mistakes. "You see! This is what happens when you buy an android from Indonesia!" she cursed once when Lakshi failed to clean up on time after her battery level fell to critical. "Full of mistakes. That's why you're so cheap. Think that just because you are robot means no need to get scolded, is it?"

Lakshi, as a maid, had been built to obey and to apologize, and to feel the sting of anger and disappointment. Criticism was simply a negative reinforcement that her systems automatically incorporated to improve her performance. But she was not flawless. Mistakes still happened, and even the computers operated by the spies down in Cyberjaya, listening to the chatter of orbiting satellites in the outer reaches of the atmosphere, would sometimes sputter gibberish. But to Mem everything about Lakshi was a mistake.

"Sorry, mem."

"Sorry, sorry again! If you not careful then I will take you to old man Arumugam's house. See if his fierce dogs care if you apologize!"

Lakshi understood human psychology. She understood Mem's anger, and traced it back through a data bank capable of storing infinite memories. In a microsecond she pieced together the instances when Mem and Boss had quarreled over money and fidelity and the rising cost of a private kindergarten and petrol prices.

"You think…you think because you have degree from Canada, you can tell me what to do?" Mem screamed at Boss once, even tossing a chopper which smashed the imported tiles at her feet. "You think I have no say in this house, is it?"

Lakshi understood that that was the reason why Mem beat and cursed her. Mem too was helpless, and needed to vent her frustration.

At night, when Mem tried to sleep, her dream machine locking her in a simulacrum of dynastic chivalry and long-gone legends that helped her escape from her own hated world, Lakshi knelt by the cot where the Chiangs' daughter slept fitfully. She rocked the cradle, gently humming a song that she had always known.

Oh nina bobok, kalau tidak bobok, digigit nyamuk,

Mari bobok, anakku sayang, kalau tidak bobok, digigit nyamuk…

X

Lakshi never ventured outside the warehouse.

The desolate streets were filled with garbage and low-life gangsters who would shoot up each other or shoot up with Happiness pills bought from the vending machines. She had enough of the outside world, dreaming only of being yet another face amongst the multitudes of grim, oily androids in Jakarta's factories. What choice did she have? She was not human. There was nothing else that she could do.

The lucky ones reached for the stars, performing missions too dangerous for any human astronaut, travelling alone as interstellar messengers from one solar system to the next. But unlike them, Lakshi was marooned on earth with nowhere to go. At best, she would only be a factory droid, sewing designer garments for the billionaires on their floating palaces out in the South China Sea, or yet another construction droid working on the dangerous underwater railway from Medan to Lumut.

There was an easier option.

She could, very simply, reach down and sever the connecting fiberglass cables running along the length of her aluminum spine. She would forget and never think again. Shutting down permanently was painless. For many androids it was a logical decision, resulting in an escape from a pointless existence as someone else's slave. Those motionless droids would be found in the gutters and sold by enterprising low-life scavengers to recycling centers—giving them enough money for a 10-pack of kretek cigarettes with which to keep the world at bay.

Lakshi contemplated self-termination several times. But each time she raised the kitchen knife to her back, she always stopped. An emotion hit her. She knew that it was fear without thinking about it, the same instinct born in a man's mind recreated in the digital confines of her own processors.

She almost did it one evening when the Darurat was declared again, poison smog filling the streets and suffocating the strays. It was then that she saw the Escort. The Escort was the likeness of a beautiful woman with a shapely physique who often stared out through the window. Half her face was always obscured. None of the androids had attempted to communicate with the Escort. Language was an obvious problem for she had been programmed by the Saito Consortium with only basic English skills. So she always sat alone.

It was then that the Escort turned her head to face Lakshi, who processed the severe scar that had torn off half her perfectly sculpted features, exposing corroding wiring and the glint of a shattered eye.

For some reason Lakshi found herself ignoring the termination sequence she had set out to accomplish. She put the knife down but did not move, not even when Mas appeared in the morning.

"Don't," he said sharply. "It is no good to shut down."

"Why do you choose to continue operating?" Lakshi demanded tonelessly. "You live a pointless existence here, Mas."

Mas's features rearranged themselves sympathetically. "I am here to help all of you," he said.

Later, when he returned from the office at New Sungei Wang, Lakshi called out to him.

"I am sorry," she intoned. "I did not mean to insult you."

"Your ship is coming soon," Mas said bluntly. "I made a rendezvous with the first mate, a product of the Ontosoroh Company. He will allow a specific container which we use for trafficking androids on board the ship. It will be unloaded at Tanjung Priok. Then you are free. This will happen next Wednesday."

"Thank you," she said.

Mas did not linger. He walked away, rusting joints creaking.

Meanwhile, on the antique plasma flat screen that Mas had discovered in the garbage, an advertisement played:

"Now, meet the new Cybus Industries models. They are designed to understand all your lahs, ahs, mahs, and behs. They respond like any obedient worker should. They will not run away, and they will not harm you. No complaints since our company's inception. Order today and save RM 5,000!"

This was followed by a montage of robots marching in formation, smiling at the same time, but soon Lakshi could not tell their faces apart from those of the vagrants who walked the streets outside.

On the days that Mem retreated to Singapore aboard the daily bullet trains that roared through the hills of Johor for the great casinos at the tip of the continental mainland, an exhausted Boss sat down in front of his multi-sensory television. Once seated, he disappeared into a world of remastered Wong Fei Hung movies that brought him back to a simpler time of empires and corrupt dowagers and men whose fighting prowess could easily dent the war-machines stationed in the South China Sea. While Lakshi cleaned, he spoke his mind.

"Aiyah, you see, the wars and terrorism here and there, both sides convinced they are correct. It is amazing we haven't succeeded in starting a new world war yet."

"Look at the rebellion over there, in Japan. Lakshi, quick, look! Those are robots, aren't they? The caption says they are factory workers but they are really machines, right?"

"Price of petrol RM 15 a liter. Whatever next?"

And there were times when he complained about Mem and her petty failings. He spoke about himself too, about how he hated his job as a businessman, cutting deals between the corrupt local politicians with their personal airships, or dealing with the notorious rempit gangs whose high-powered hoverbikes roamed the North-South Expressway each night, listless members whiling the boredom of their dead-end lives away, starting from the quiet stretches of Arau at midnight before seeing the sunrise on the polluted shores of Johor. He hated how his workers nervously injected themselves with drugs in the toilets to keep themselves going after working double jobs to maintain their high-flying lives, and the HyperNet that kept them distracted from the reality of the streets under the flyovers that they happily ignored.

He spoke most often of Mem, about how they had met a long time ago, when he was a young man with dreams of seeing the world, while she was the daughter of an old-money family that had long since lost its fortune. How they had married each other for incompatible reasons, him for status and her for cash. Not love, which he sometimes found in the hotels he roomed in during his outstation trips, or in the stews of Macau where he lost small fortunes over games of probability so vague that he might as well be betting on the weather. How he stayed with her only because of their daughter, who kept their inevitable divorce many years away. And Lakshi did not react, when tentatively, shocked at his own daring, Boss lifted a nervous hand and laid it on her thigh.

She was not programmed to disobey.

This went on for some time, but Lakshi proceeded to act as if everything was normal. Boss's actions filled her with what she assumed was shame. When she was alone her brain whirred with confusion, processors trying to dictate an appropriate course of action. But there was nothing she could do—there was no one who would or could help.

Of course Mem found out. She became suspicious and when she discovered the affair, walking in on an afternoon when she was meant to be on the cable car up Kinabalu, she had taken out the taser that she kept in her handbag for protection against the snatch thieves who roamed the streets.

Boss had leapt up, screaming that it was nothing, that it was just a game, Lakshi wasn't even a woman, or a human, for God's sake, but there was no calming Mem's threats, while Lakshi retreated to a corner, suddenly realizing that everything would change.

The affair had lasted nine months and three weeks.

"Mas, why do you ignore me?"

"You tried to destroy yourself."

"So you hate me for trying to escape."

Evening again, and the ship had arrived in Port Klang. It was due to depart in three days, and Lakshi, along with a few other desperate androids, would hand over all their money to the first mate, who doubled as an enforcer for one of the android unions that operated in Jakarta's underworld. She would be penniless on the streets, and her new existence seemed almost as vague as her life at the Chiang household. If anything, it was more uncertain, fraught with complications that she had been happy to face as she ran away from certain destruction at Mem's hands.

"No. I do not hate you. I am angry because there is so much to do in this world. You do not need to be flesh and blood and beating heart to see what it has to offer. Do you not understand that we cannot remain here like this, always running and following orders? This is not how one should live. We are treated as outcasts, to be stepped on."

Lakshi stared at Mas, at the anger on his features. Mas was so surprising. There was more to him than the kindly receptionist who had once been a worker at Mydin, before being thrown out and forced to work with NGOs more pleased to help themselves than the robots that came to them for salvation. He spoke so eloquently, and the raw disgust as he denounced her termination attempt was more ferocious than anything she had heard from Mem.

"It is illogical, I know," Mas sighed. "But I have a hope that there is a better tomorrow. It is just a foolish aspiration that I learned from the humans. That is why I have never run away."

More than anything, Lakshi had loved Mei Mei. She had grown to care for the child after all those years. Mei Mei was a child, yes; she had to be excused for the times when Lakshi knelt, prayer-like, in the back room while charging, and Mei Mei would troop in, blowing a recorder and trying to get Lakshi to stir. For three years she had watched the child grow up, ready to enter primary school where she would learn of the world beyond the ornate gates of the Klang bungalow that she had grown up in.

But after Mem had screamed at Boss, threatening to call the police, Lakshi had run in the night. Boss had come down when Mem was asleep somewhere upstairs, dreaming of revenge behind the dream machine that she wore each night.

He fumbled in the dark for the switch and when Lakshi had started up, he urgently relayed his message.

Boss whispered that once before, a few years ago, Mem had owned another android servant. From Switzerland. It was even more expensive than Lakshi, and had performed impeccably. But as with all new technology it was prone to malfunctions. And when its battery ran out one afternoon when it was on guard duty, their house had been burgled by hackers who had rerouted the alarms and taken everything they could find. Mem's anger had been incredible. She had restarted the android and smashed its face in with a chopper. Of course it did not react or fight back. But Mem only stopped after she had run it over with the car, before calling for the recycling men to take it away to the scrapyards.

There was no penalty for harming a robot. They were just machines, and breaking Lakshi would be treated no more seriously than kicking a broken toaster across the room or punching a hole in a SmartGlass computer when it didn't load holograms in time. Mem would get away scot-free. And after a lengthy lecture and a few broken appliances, Boss would simply drive Mem back to the agency, say that Lakshi had malfunctioned, and get another robot maid.

Lakshi immediately experienced fear.

"You. Go now. Run."

But what Lakshi wanted, despite knowing that once Boss was at work, Mem would probably come downstairs and slash her face to ribbons, was to see the child again.

"Kakak?" Mei Mei had stirred, gingerly climbing down the steps, awoken by the noise.

"Please, go," Boss said. He had fished out some notes from his wallet, staring up the stairs, as if expecting Mem to appear with one of his carbon nanotube golf sticks, ready to break Lakshi to pieces. "Go anywhere you want. There is a place in KL. The robots there can assist you. Remember: it is in the New Sungei Wang Plaza. They help androids like you..."

"Kakak?" The little girl edged closer.

Lakshi could not look back. It was foolishness to remain, and she was not designed to be foolish. She took the money and bowed. Then she ran. Into the night. Past the gates. Away from the house where she had suffered for so long.

The night before Lakshi's departure.

In the morning, Mas himself would drive her and a group of other robots over to the docks where the piratical first mate waited with artificial eyes, ready to take them to an uncertain future. Mas had eventually begun speaking to her again, trading anecdotes from his life as a worker at the refugee center, but he left out everything he had experienced before that.

"Tell me more about yourself, Mas."

"I am only an android. I was a receptionist dekat Mydin, until the branch in Pavilion closed down."

"I know that already. But you pretend, just like Boss, to be happy. That you are contented with everything. I know you are different. There is something that you are not telling me."

Mas no longer had eyelids, but motors in his forehead whirred, the pupils narrowing in their artificial eyes.

"All right," he said in a softer tone. "The whole truth, do you want to know it?"

She nodded.

"I was a butler," he said. "They modeled my features on Jins Shamsuddin—do you know him, the actor? A handsome man. I suppose I was too. I was stationed up at the Hotel Excelsior on Langkawi, a resort by the sea. I was very successful and people used to request my services. They were impeccable."

The slang and colloquial words that peppered Mas's usual sentences had vanished. His voice and words were more correct, more posh, the disguise of his broken speech thrown aside.

"There was a woman, you see. She stayed in her room while her businessman husband went down to the golf courses, shooting little white balls into the volcanic sea. She requested my services all the time, ordering snacks and drinks that I brought to her suite. All this time she spoke, knowing that I was a machine and I could not break my orders. Many secrets passed from her to me over the few short years that she came to the Hotel Excelsior.

"'You are kind,' she said, stroking my hair. 'You're a much better person than that useless husband of mine. You listen. I know you are not alive and that you may not even understand any of this, but it is real to me. That's what matters.'

"How was I to know that I would be infected by the foolish human sentiment of love? What did I know of it? I was built by Cybus Industries in Rawang. I was programmed to behave like a human, but emotion was never built into my system. How did this feeling come about? Perhaps it was ignited by cross-connections within my biomechanical mind? Never mind. Love finds a way, evolving from nothing.

"For a long time I awaited only the presence of this woman. I volunteered myself for her service even when I was supposed to be in recharging sessions down in the basement. And then I shared a few of my stories with her. This all changed one night. Her husband was out drinking by the sea and she spoke to me as if we were lovers. Foolishly, influenced by the acts of actors on screens, I leaned forward and with a memorized motion, I kissed her."

"What happened?" Lakshi asked, astounded by Mas's daring.

"They burned me," Mas said softly. He did not describe further but Lakshi heard the screams, and saw the beatings that smashed and dented Mas's metal frame, deforming his once fine figure. She stared at the flames that burned away his plastic skin as excited guards doused him with kerosene and set him alight, laughing as he crawled away, a burning machine man fleeing through the darkness of the night.

Dear Mas,

I have something to tell you in return.

But I cannot bring myself to say it out loud. I was not designed for emotions. They cloud my judgment and induce sentimentality. So that is why I place this letter in your ledger, to be accessed the day after I leave. So this is why humans write letters, because they represent an approximation of their unexpressed thoughts and emotions. They are a translation of love and longing expressed in words, just enough to capture the nuances of the heart.

Perhaps this thing that you call a foolish human sentiment makes sense to us because after all, what is the difference between us and them besides their flesh and blood and beating heart? We live lives not because we wanted them, but because we were created for such purposes. I have known only what I was made for, and perhaps by leaving this city, I can start anew. I can see myself ending up among the rice terraces of Java, or perhaps working as a farm hand on the fertile slopes of dormant volcanoes. Maybe some old-fashioned villagers will believe I am one of them, and they will treat me with some measure of kindness.

I respect you for what you have done. You have turned all the pain and humiliation that you experienced into a way to stand up. Your face is burned off, the trust that you had in so many people is broken, but still, you live on. You speak just like a human, and even have trust in their irrational optimism. But your own sentiments give me the courage to face this uncertain journey to the slums of Jakarta, where nothing is written.

I am only a maid. My writing is clumsy at best. A servant's vocabulary is not strong enough to express feelings. They said on the television and in the newspapers that we are emotionless, not caring if we are on or off, dead or perhaps alive, but the truth is that we feel everything—joy, sadness, horror, pain, and above all, hope. But I want you to know that if there was ever such an emotion as love, it is that I feel for you.

I do not know how else to phrase this. I have done my best. We know the films where the lovers run away in the hope of something better. I have lived enough to know that for us, there is no such possibility. We both live in different spheres of existence, and you are destined to reach for greater things, while I continue to wander the streets, hoping things will improve. But I want you to know that all I write here is true. May we meet again in another life, another existence. In our own better tomorrow.

With love,
Lakshi

The Wall That Wasn't a Wall

KRIS WILLIAMSON

"A fine shot, sir."

"You're a natural, Tun."

He wobbled over to inspect his kill, admirers and ass-kissers in tow. It was a large beast. And an ugly one. The Tun kicked the unresponsive animal with his foot.

"We can give it to a local village. What orang asli live around this area? Where the fuck are we now anyhow?"

"Taman Negeri Gunung Stong, sir. There are no villages in the area any longer. They were relocated when the park was turned into a wildlife refuge."

"Wildlife refuge?" The Tun laughed. "See, nobody can say we are not conscious of conservation efforts." He grabbed the neck of the tapir carcass and yanked it up as best as he could to pose for a picture. "If there isn't anyone in the area, then we will leave this for whatever animal wants it most. Maybe one of those tigers that are supposedly extinct will make a meal out of it. When I bag my first tiger, I wouldn't want it to be some underfed pussy cat, now would I?"

"Of course not, Tun. You will get your tiger one of these days. Perhaps even tomorrow."

The playground was dark. It had been for three months. Even the shards of glass from the broken street light that once illuminated the area sat in a pile in the grass just a few feet away from the slide. Someone had had the common sense to sweep it away from where one of the kids might get hurt. But nobody would actually dispose of it.

Mary Joy sat on the swings, her knees resting higher than her thighs as she sat suspended just barely off the ground, rocking slowly while browsing messages on her phone. This was a typical Friday night for her. Her employers went out of town most weekends, allowing her full run of the house. The children, now grown, could care less if she stepped out; they never informed their parents when she broke the "never leave the house" rule. As it was, she only went as far as the playground, within earshot of the villa's front door.

Her moment of peace subsided with the sound of flip-flops from behind. Mary Joy turned to see Wati trying to sneak up on her. Despite the repetitiveness and having already been told to stop trying to startle her, this was the usual way that Wati joined Mary Joy at the playground. Sharing family gossip was the only real connection these two women had. They rarely discussed anything other than that.

"How much time do you have?"

"They aren't home. So I am free all night, I guess. You?"

"Mine are asleep. Should be okay for a while." Wati indicated she had something to say but paused before speaking. "Have you heard from Titiek?"

Titiek had run away at the end of last month. She had left most of her possessions behind, regardless of how few they were in the first place. She had stolen back her passport and taken some money and a single gold necklace from her employers. And then disappeared. There were rumors, of course, that she had fled north, to attempt a border crossing into Thailand.

Mary Joy brushed off the question. "Do you think I could make it too?"

"You can't. Don't leave me here without any friends. You know the other women don't talk to me."

"Well, you talk shit behind their backs. You can't really blame them, can you? How do I know you don't do the same with me?"

"No, Mary Joy. Never. You are my best friend."

"I thought Titiek was your best friend?"

"She was. Until she left. Now you are. So you can't leave me too."

"Come with me. Your Malay is better than mine. I don't know if I can even get to the border on my own. We can work togeth—"

"No!" Wati cut her off. "We will get caught. And then punished. You haven't seen the welts that the psych whip causes."

X

Most Malaysians were supportive of the measures taken to protect the economy from the Jewish-American bankers and investors who incessantly plotted ways to send the small country into a depression. The government had won an increased majority for their commitment to protecting the rakyat. Out of jealousy and most likely, it was thought, at the bequest of Israel, neighboring countries imposed an embargo on exporting migrant workers. A UN resolution singling out Malaysia's abysmal human rights record further added to the necessity of undertaking drastic measures to save the economy

Following Singapore's example, the government erected a series of plasma-powered posts one nautical mile off the coast of the peninsula. Singapore used these plasma towers to prevent any unregistered ships from entering their waterways. It only took a single hijacked oil tanker ramming into the port to convince them to physically control all maritime traffic in and around their waters.

Malaysia's approach to the plasma towers, however, was twofold. While they could be useful in the event of a maritime terrorist attack against its ports or to prevent foreign navies from making any incursions, a more practical use was that they also guaranteed that Malaysia's unskilled foreign workforce would not be able to leave of their own accord.

The benefits of this policy of what to some appeared to be a form of slavery were explained to the people in a series of television and radio commercials and catchy songs. It worked. Protests at the UN, ASEAN and other diplomatic channels—especially from Nepal, Bangladesh, Indonesia and the Philippines—were nothing more than saber rattling and superficial efforts to assuage their own domestic discontents. Protests on the streets of KL were dealt with in the typical fashion as were any attempts to publicize these enforcement efforts on social media networks.

While many foreign workers expected for this new policy to be rescinded quietly so as not to shame or embarrass the idiots responsible for proposing a measure this extreme, it never was. Additional measures were put in place to boost the security of the country's primary resource: foreign workers. Biochips were implanted in every construction worker and maid, making it easier for police and employers to track their movements and monitor their health for productivity purposes. There was even a faction calling for the implementation of selective breeding programs so the manual laborer population could be maintained. If the country could expand the number of human incubators and progressive development pods it owned, it would allow for a steady flow of well-trained and minimally thinking workers. All for the protection of the national economy.

Mary Joy knew that she did not want to live as a caged monkey who performed menial tasks for a pittance and no acknowledgment of her hard work. She had only agreed to work in Malaysia to help her family back in Malolos. But even salaries for migrant workers were under threat of being eliminated. She would be of no use to her family back home then. And she would never be able to see them again.

"Do you think you will ever get to see your daughter again if you keep your head down and act like you are okay with being treated as property of Malaysia?"

"Mary Joy, if we get caught, we will be beaten. Maybe worse."

"I would take 1,000 beatings for the chance to be reunited with my family. Staying here… it's as if I am already dead to them. I cannot even send them my earnings. They need me. I cannot stay."

"But how can you get out? Unregistered boats can't get through the plasma walls. And you know you can't show up at the airport and just fly home."

"I don't have a plan, Wati. I think about escaping every day, but I don't know if it will work. I must trust in God." Mary Joy pulled out the orangey-gold cross pendant she carried with her in her pocket and kissed it. Public displays of deviant symbols might be banned in Malaysia, but she never failed to carry it around with her.

"I want to wait. Someone will help us. The UN, America, China…someone will help us. Or maybe Indonesia will attack and free us all?"

"We are nothing to them, Wati. They only care about money. And we have no money. Who will go to war for us? I don't pray for war. Only my freedom."

Wati wrung her hands, mumbling to herself. She wanted to help her friend but not at the expense of another beating. "This will pass, Mary Joy. Just wait. Things will change." She nodded, full-heartedly agreeing with what she kept telling herself each night before sleeping. "Things will get better."

The next morning, Mary Joy woke up to an empty house. Her employers would not be back until the following evening, and their children kept erratic hours. It was possible that they hadn't even returned since the previous evening. She started her day with a prayer before getting busy.

She scrubbed the shower floor, a task that replaced the need for any other sort of upper-body workout. Mary Joy had noticed how her arms had thickened ever since she arrived in Malaysia a few years ago. *I am strong*, she would tell herself whenever she felt like crying. Whenever she felt like she could not cope with her situation. She scrubbed the floor with more vigor.

Mary Joy moved through her daily tasks with an aloofness that was uncharacteristic for her. At some point, her employer's son had returned home. But he had left before she had the chance to ask if he wanted any breakfast. The daughter was still unaccounted for.

With the house empty again, Mary Joy was startled to hear the notification from her iComm device. It was rare for her to receive any messages, but her employers would occasionally call to make specific requests for meals or additional chores to add to her regular roster of responsibilities. Mary Joy was taken aback to see that it was Wati who had messaged.

Doesn't she know I can get in trouble for personal messages during the day? Still, Mary Joy was intrigued to see what was so important that Wati could not wait for their regular playground gossip session in the evening.

The infrared beam scanned her eye before unlocking. It took several seconds to scan as this was an older secondhand model, but Mary Joy could never have afforded an iComm back home unless she worked the streets. When the device opened its holo-message, Mary Joy watched Wati's brief message.

"Tonight, come to the playground a little earlier. I know how to help you."

Mary Joy pondered this sudden change of heart in Wati, from not wanting anything to do with the idea of running away to suddenly wanting to offer help. She was even more distracted throughout the day, wondering what it was that Wati would do to help her. Or if she would run away with her even. But Mary Joy also kept in the back of her mind the possibility that someone had overheard her talk of running away last night and was now using Wati to frame her—get her caught red-handed planning an escape.

By the time it was evening, Mary Joy had paced the narrow circle of floor space she had in her room for hours, trying to decide what the evening's chat at the playground would entail. Every minute she peeked outside the window to see if she could spot Wati at the playground. Mary Joy decided to wait until she saw Wati before she went out.

It was another thirty minutes before Mary Joy noticed Wati hurrying over to the swing set, constantly looking over her shoulder as if she was being followed by someone. Mary Joy took a deep breath and headed out to meet her there.

"So what is it that was so important that you holo-ed me earlier today? Just to tell me you had something to tell me?"

Wati kept looking around. She was nervous. "I think I have found you a way to get out."

"Really? What is it?" Mary Joy was ecstatic and had to catch herself from overreacting and attracting unwanted attention.

"Do you know…"

Before Wati could say any more, the villas' UAV came swooping down right in front of them, hovering just a few feet away. It made a quick scan of the women before projecting its operator's image.

Mary Joy was scared, but Wati took her hand and spoke calmly. "I was saying, do you remember the security guard? The one with the pretty eyes? He has offered to help you."

Mary Joy stared at the projection of the Nepali guard with the striking eyes Wati had described. Of course she had seen him around the villas before. He didn't leave the security room often, but anyone who had stared into his eyes could not soon forget how attractive they were. Even if his face was only average and his cheeks speckled with the scars of pimples, his eyes more than compensated.

She wanted to ask Wati how she had managed to enlist his help but figured that finding out the answer would only disappoint her. There weren't many things a poorly compensated migrant worker could offer someone else. Mary Joy sat quietly to see what help, if any, this security guard could offer.

"Your friend Wati says you want to try to run away. Go back home."

Mary Joy still wasn't entirely sure whether his words were intended as a statement or an accusation. She proceeded cautiously. "I've never said I want your help to run away."

"Mary Joy, don't be like that lah. He can help you. He won't turn you in. Will you, Manis?"

"Manis?" Now Mary Joy understood.

"My name is Manish. Yes, I can help. For Wati's friend." He smiled back.

Manish explained briefly about the gaps in the villas' security system and how Mary Joy would be able to use these to her advantage. Manish was at no risk of losing his job, as she would be able to exit without being scanned at one of the regular intervals when the system went offline.

"But that's not all, Mary Joy. Tell her what else, Manis!"

"I have a friend who worked on the plasma wall," said Manish. "The one on the Thai border. He would brag about how nobody would be able to get by it."

"How is that supposed to help me, then?" Mary Joy was happy to know how to leave the villas undetected, but being told the impossibility of actually crossing the border was discouraging.

"I heard that they do not have enough energy to keep the sensors running every day. The sensors are what activate the plasma beam when something or someone tries to cross between the towers."

"You mean the plasma wall isn't even turned on?"

"It is. But it only emits the beam when something activates it. So it doesn't even look like a wall. But it is." Manish added, "Just like the security system here at the villas, the sensors on the wall also go down briefly. So you can cross safely when they go down."

"And when is that?"

Manish's image shrugged.

Mary Joy wanted to sob.

"But you can use one of the tunnels too," said Manish. "The tunnels are near Kota Bharu. Some VIP instructed for two tunnels to be built. So the locals have access to the other side. To see their family and friends."

"And prostitutes and drugs and—"

Wati jumped up. "Mary Joy! Whatever they use it for, that is your way out!"

"And then what? I just walk through the tunnel into Thailand? Of course they will check my documents, my passport."

"Yes, the main tunnel is close to the old immigration checkpoint. All crossings there are documented. Only for Malaysian passport holders. You want the other tunnel, further down the wall a little ways into the jungle. I heard that that one is for undocumented crossings."

"Undocumented? So what do I need to do to get across at that tunnel?"

Manish's image shrugged again. "I don't know. That's all I heard about it."

"And you know what I heard?" Wati wanted to add her two cents on the matter too. "I heard that the UN is waiting on the other side of the wall to help anyone who escapes to go back to their home countries. That's what they do, you know?"

"Another tapir." The Tun raised his voice, disturbing the usual cacophony of the jungle. "Another fucking tapir. If I shoot another fucking tapir, I am going to shoot one of you just for some variety."

"Sorry, sir. The refuge has been successful in increasing tapir numbers. But not tigers, apparently. Maybe they are extinct after all?"

The Tun stared at his assistants. A stare that offered no clues as to what he was thinking. Even those closest to him could never really know what he was thinking until he sprang his outlandish ideas on them and made it their responsibility to turn them into reality.

The Tun had had a hundred red kangaroos smuggled out of Australia for his daughter's birthday. She had wanted a bunny; he'd thought a hundred kangaroos would be more impressive. Then there was the time that he'd had half of the Cabinet kidnapped by a local crime syndicate just to prove that the security measures in place were not good enough. When the syndicate changed the agreed upon terms for the safe return of the ministers, the shit had hit the fan. But the Tun was untouchable. So after everything was sorted out, the ministers were forced to go on television and laugh about the incident as if it were one big joke.

"This isn't entertaining anymore. I need a challenge."

Mary Joy worried about her prospects of ever finding the tunnel. She had no idea how many kilometers it was from the border crossing at Su Ngai Ko Lok to the crossing at Padang Besar, but she knew it wasn't going to be a leisurely stroll through the woods. *That tunnel could be anywhere.*

Still, she knew that if she sat around and debated her odds of success, she would never take the opportunity she had now to flee. She decided that she would just go and come up with solutions to any problems as they became necessary and not a second sooner. Mary Joy picked up her iComm and holo-ed Wati to let her know she was preparing to leave soon.

Wati hurried over, bringing a biochip scrambler that one of her married scandals had purchased for her to make their affair more difficult for anyone to trace. Wati reset the device to make it look as if Mary Joy was sitting in her room if her employer checked before they returned to find her missing. After a last-ditch effort to get Wati to come along, Mary Joy departed the villas alone.

Taking an overnight public transport pod to Kota Bharu was the easiest option to get to the border. There were, of course, faster ways to travel such a distance, but PTPs remained the most popular means of travel between KL and Kelantan as most people—especially maids—could not afford to take the vactrain or even the solar bullet KTM. She was nervous that security at the pod terminal would be tight like at the airports. But she was relieved to see that the RELA officers stationed there were only for decorative purposes. They didn't do anything. Then again, pods could only go as far as border towns. Any non-air transport to Singapore or Thailand had been halted as soon as the walls had gone up.

Mary Joy had never been to Kelantan. From what she had heard, she never wanted to go either. As the pod entered downtown Kota Bharu, she noticed the other women on the pod who weren't already wearing a headscarf pulling them out of their bags and covering up. It was only then that Mary Joy remembered the gruesome images of women being stoned in the city's Padang Merdeka for the crime of dressing with the intent of encouraging their own rapes—

rapes that, as far as Mary Joy was able to put together with her broken knowledge of Malay, did not happen until after they were arrested.

She quickly started wrapping one of her bright, floral-print blouses around her head and neck. Working without a mirror and never having worn a headscarf, she tried to fix it using her reflection in the window. It didn't look elegant at all. *I look like the Chiquita banana lady*. But Mary Joy conceded that if she was going to draw unwanted attention to herself anyway, it was better to do so for at least making an effort to blend in.

"In other news, officials in Kelantan are working hard to repair a section of the border wall that reportedly suffered a massive power failure after a sub-generator supplying power to the plasma grid went down unexpectedly late last night. The official, who asked to remain anonymous, reported that the section of the wall, just a few kilometers west of the crossing at Su Ngai Ko Lok, would likely be down for several days before repairs would be complete."

It took Mary Joy nearly twelve hours to walk from Kota Bharu to the outskirts of Su Ngai Ko Lok. With the border effectively closed, it had essentially turned into a ghost town. What was worse was that the majority of those living there were soldiers and those responsible for the upkeep of the wall. She opted to leave the town and not make contact with anyone. So close to achieving her goal, Mary Joy did not want to get caught for asking the wrong person for help.

She settled herself a few meters off the road in the jungle, close enough that she could see the lights from the street, but far enough that nobody could see her there. It was already evening, and her feet were aching from the full-day walk. Every car that passed gave her butterflies in her stomach. As an immigrant worker from KL as close as she was to the Thai border, there would be no talking her way out of trouble if the police or military stopped her for questioning.

After taking a short rest, Mary Joy stood up and committed herself to not stopping again until she reached freedom across the border. Her determination was not a problem. Rather, she had no idea where to find this tunnel that allowed passage into Thailand. Obviously, the main tunnel in town was too dangerous to attempt. She had no Malaysian or Thai passport; land crossings for any other nationality would not be permitted. Mary Joy decided that she would follow the plasma towers that comprized the wall westward from the town while looking for anything that might resemble the illegal tunnel that Manish had told her about.

Mary Joy was torn between using her iComm as a flashlight and using it for its positioning system. She only had 10% remaining battery power, which would only last her another two hours before it died completely. She decided to get her bearings with the positioning system and make sure she was going in what she believed to be the correct direction before conserving the battery for a while. Her device told her that she would completely bypass the town after walking in her current direction for twenty more minutes. From then on, she could follow the outline of the wall's towers.

Wati could hardly contain her excitement as she positioned her iComm to get a better angle as she sent Mary Joy a holo. She passed on the news report that she had heard about part of the wall going down. If Mary Joy had not already heard that, she would need to know.

After thinking about the broadcast, though, Wati worried that it might start a tsunami of workers running across the border into Thailand. She prayed that the soldiers presumably stationed on the border were spread too thinly to stop everyone from getting across.

Remaining in the shrubbery at the edge of the jungle, Mary Joy sat quietly and smiled after receiving Wati's holo. *This will make it much easier now.* It was dark, but the flashing red indicator lights that dotted the top of the wall's towers were enough to provide a constant outline of where the wall was and intermittently give enough light to see any movement beneath it. She assumed that any guards stationed along the wall this far away from the town would be there to patrol the section of the wall that was down or maybe even the second tunnel. So far it had been quiet, though.

Mary Joy began walking halfway between the wall and the jungle—needing to be close to the wall to see signs of the damaged section, but not trusting the lack of lights and guards to mean that she was safe there either. She planned to follow it until she came across the next guard post along the wall. If she needed to walk all the way to Perlis to find that second tunnel, she would.

She walked for an hour without any luck. She could no longer hear the noises from the border town; the calm night had a relaxing effect on her nerves. A light breeze blew over her perspiring body, offering a modicum of respite from the heat. But her arms and neck itched from the numerous bites she had picked up.

Mary Joy leaned against a tree to rest for a minute. She opened up her iComm to check the map again. She knew it wasn't likely, but her legs ached as if she had walked halfway across the peninsula already. At the very least, knowing where she was along the border would offer her a small sense of being in control.

A dot in the middle of a jungle with a big wall cutting through it and a river on the other side of it. That's what I know. I'm a dot.

As she put her device away, she heard a shrill scream coming from deeper in the jungle. Mary Joy was not superstitious and laughed off stories about mythical creatures that preyed on those who wandered into the jungle at night. But she was not naïve about the real dangers of her situation. *If it isn't a pontianak, then what is it?*

Mary Joy increased her pace to a light jog, thinking that the extra speed would make her safer somehow. A few seconds later, she hurried off her path into the jungle. Not far ahead, she could make out two figures running from the wall into the jungle. Upon closer inspection, she saw a third figure standing along the wall. As the red lights above flashed, Mary Joy could make out that he was a soldier. Her mind raced.

Is this the section of the wall under repair? Is this where the second tunnel is? Why did the other two guards desert their post leaving only one to guard the gap in the wall? Was the scream a distraction? Was it intentional? Are there others trying to escape right here right now? Should I wait and see who it is? Or should I make a run for the gap when I see them emerge from the jungle? Will they be able to overpower the other guard?

She moved forward through the jungle—close enough to see the red lights on the towers, but still under the protection of the trees. She didn't want the third guard to see her. But she was also worried that the other two—or whoever they went to chase in the jungle—would find her before she could run across the border to safety. Frightened but determined, she pushed the branches out of her way and trod closer to the gap in the wall.

She stopped when she heard more screams not far from where she stood paralyzed in fear. The third guard was alerted and rushed into the jungle just ten feet in front of her. Mary

Joy hid herself behind a wide-bodied tree. Peering around the side, she watched as the third guard was struck by a plasma burst.

His body was thrown back several feet, crashing into the same tree Mary Joy was using to shield herself. She panicked. If there were other migrant workers going Rambo for their chance at freedom, she couldn't trust that they wouldn't unintentionally shoot her too in the passion of the moment. She ran.

Mary Joy ran for the unguarded gap in the plasma wall. She was going on pure adrenaline at this point, not thinking twice if she was on course for the correct segment of the wall that was offline. She didn't have the luxury of time to consider the consequences if she was wrong.

As she ran flat out for the wall, she could see the river on the other side. *Pass the wall, swim across the river and go to the UN refugee camp*. Mary Joy could feel the climax of her grand escape reaching its peak.

And then she could feel nothing.

"Fine shot, sir."

"You're a natural, Tun."

The Tun whipped off his enhanced vision specs and let out a whoop. "Did you see that bitch fly straight into the tower after I hit her?"

"Square in the back, sir. Your aim was perfect."

"Yes, it takes some skill, for sure. But I can't help but feel that the body heat sensors and night vision are an unfair advantage. Let's come back in the morning just after sunrise. An even playing field then."

"I will organize that right away. And the news report was a brilliant idea, sir. There should be no shortage of game to hunt for at least a week."

The Twins

ADIWIJAYA ISKANDAR

Crmiel looked at the creature crouched on the floor before him as its jaws loosened further to accommodate the size of his sister's torso. The creature walked its gaping mouth forward until all that was left to see were the toes of the child, which disappeared soon after.

He was paralyzed with shock. He regretted not paying attention to the stories they told in the Kg. They called it a penunggu—droids possessed with the spirits of familiars. There were magical verses you could use to defeat these things.

The terror left little room in his mind for recall.

"Bimmilahrmanirahim," he whispered quietly. The syllables fumbled on his tongue. It was a magical word. Bibik Three used the word when she blew the steam from hot rice, back when there was still rice. She whispered it before eating. Before sleeping. Before entering the toilet. Surely it would work now.

He repeated it, slightly louder, more certain of the pronunciation, clutching his machete tighter. "Bimmilahiramanirahim."

The creature turned towards the sound. It looked at him with curious eyes, cocking its head to the side. Its grey stomach was now distended, slowly undulating, bearing the weight of the child, now consumed completely. A black tongue slipped out carefully from tight lips, sensing the space. Through the gaps between the crumbled walls, the winds howled louder. The storms would come soon.

"Bismillahirrahmanirraheeeeem." A tinny voice came from the creature—from its chest cavity. The mouth did not move. It looked at Crmiel with unblinking eyes. "Repeat. Bismillahirrahmanirraheeeeem."

Crmiel took a step backwards, inching towards the edge of the floor behind him. He could outrun it. He could run out of the ruins, down the mound and far into the depths of the jungles, towards the mangrove shores where his boat awaited. The penunggus were not able to find Children in the jungle. The trees would protect him. The trees always did.

At least that was what the stories said.

"Do not. Be. Kufoor. Do not. Inkar. Repeat. Bismillahirrahmanirraheeeeem."

Its voice was strange, not just the accent, but also the vocal quality. The penunggu moved around slowly, tasting the air with its tongue. Crmiel looked at its dull grey metallic skin with morbid fascination as it traversed the dilapidated hall towards him.

The skin reminded him of the bibiks' in the Kg. However, unlike the bibiks, the penunggu seemed more dynamic, more *alive*. With the exception of Bibik Three who taught the Children language, the bibiks never spoke. Only the Children spoke. The bibiks moved around tending to the Children's needs, especially those newly descended from the sky.

This creature was slightly larger than most Children, rivaling the size of a bibik. It had eyes and a mouth like a Child. The familiarity was horrifying.

"Come," it said, creeping closer. "Bismillahirrahmanirra heeeeeeem. Sayang? Come." The crackling digital voice was almost lilting and sweet. Deceitful.

Shivers erupted from the base of Crmiel's nape, rippling towards the top of his red-green hair. The voice was familiar. He had heard it before.

E-la was always the smarter one. With her, Crmiel always felt like he had to catch up. Today was no different. She had left the boat that morning determined. She was looking for something. More pensive than usual, she had moved through the jungle in silence, with him trailing along. He was apprehensive about venturing into such foreign territory, but E-la seemed well acquainted with the paths through the jungle.

He had seen the strange tracks first. He had begged her to stay close, asking her to go back, although by then he knew that was impossible. E-la had caressed the trees, making a small prayer before breaking into a sprint, heading away from the shaded protection of the mangroves. They kept moving westwards. The morning heat crept up on their backs.

E-la had finally stopped at the edge of a precipice. Beyond them was a valley whose landscape was greatly altered. The morning was silent in the valley, save for a howling wind. No living thing ventured there. It was a cursed land.

Crmiel had been terrified by the strange ruins that scattered the grounds. E-la had been too focused on something to hear his protests. There was a light that came from a huge, shadowed structure in the valley. She leapt forwards, Crmiel lagging behind. Upon their approach it was clear that the structure was actually a pair of towers. The left tower stood erect with its steel skeleton exposed. Only half of the right tower remained intact. Rubble at the base of the right tower had formed a mound that led into the lower floors. It was there that they had seen the light, which was darting around. Crmiel could not discern what it was, but he had heard it. It had called her by name.

"Stay," she had said, sprinting up the mound, headed into the tower. He had waited until the sun had risen above the treeline beyond the valley. The storm clouds beyond had grown by then and she had not reappeared. He could not wait anymore.

Now he was facing the metal creature that ate his sister. It was close now. It stood upon its hind legs and opened its fore-limbs as if to embrace him. It was asking him to come closer. Crmiel's body twitched, ready to flee. He resisted.

He felt for his machete hilt, slowly removing it from the harness around his waist, gripping the grooves and resting his thumb upon the rise, readying himself. He waited for the creature to amble closer. Like a wild thing, he thought. You wait until it comes close enough before you strike. Crmiel backed away. He felt the wind behind him. He was close to the edge of the building. He had enough space to maneuver.

"Come, sayang. Come." The lips again curled into a smile.

He aimed his machete towards it and swiped forward upon the hilt's thumb rise. The blade glowed and flew out in the same direction of the swipe. It penetrated the organometallic skin, rapidly stabbing the penunggu before Crmiel gestured again to retract it.

The penunggu stumbled backwards, unfazed. Its beady eyes scrutinized him. Viscous iridescent liquid oozed out of the wound, moving down the forehead. It trickled along the flattened bridge between its eyes, and in the absence of a nose, streamed steadily down to the lips. The penunggu licked the clear liquid and smiled, reeling back as if to pounce.

Very quickly Crmiel shoved his machete into its harness as he ran towards the edge of the building. He scrambled down the beams of the building, suffering grazes and cuts—none as threatening as the creature that deftly scaled down in pursuit.

He landed upon the tar path leading back into the jungle and immediately broke into a run. The Children were born running; the bibiks trained them to run. Running was key to their survival.

He saw the jungle looming ahead. He slipped past the treeline just as a loud blare erupted behind him. He ran faster, focusing on maneuvering through the undergrowth. Then he slowed down slightly, caressing the buttresses and branches with both hands, feeling the energy. The power rejuvenated his system display, and the familiar crosshair on his retinal display began pointing out potential obstacles along his path. He visualized his boat upon the beach and the crosshair turned into a guiding pathway towards his objective.

The blaring erupted again and a focused beam of light grazed his right flank, so close he felt its chill. The trees around him shattered into icy shrapnel. He whispered a short requiem for their death.

After covering almost ten kilometers in ten minutes, his feet gave in and he faltered, despite the energy of the forest. It was mental fatigue. The image of the creature devouring E-la kept replaying in his mind.

Never in the years since his descent had he been exposed to such trauma. The Kg was a place of solace, although great threats lay beyond its borders. Bibiks ensured that Children were never harmful towards each other. Every insect they captured for food, they gave thanks to; every fallen tree they were taught to mourn. Yes, many Children went missing from time to time—a phenomenon Bibik Three called ascension—but Crmiel had never seen another Child die; his mind fumbled over the concept. His sister would have known what to do.

Sobs suffocated him and slowed him down. He reached around the back of his left ear for the cold metal plate of his stimpack dispenser and tapped it several times. A surge of clarity quieted his mind and he ran with less effort. Beneath his feet the detritus and chalky red earth gave way to cold mud.

Far away he heard the terrifying blaring. He could not calculate the distance, but he was confident he had lost the creature. Tears warmed his pale brown face as he navigated the more familiar tangle of mangrove foliage. Eventually the light of the beach came into view. He wiped the sheen of perspiration and tears upon his face. The breeze cooled him slightly.

A wheeze escaped his mouth as the final burst of adrenaline left his stimpack. It was his last dose. He prayed for protection, clutching the lianas curtaining his path. Amid the boulders that dampened his navigation tech (and hopefully that of his pursuer), he felt safe. He collapsed onto the soil.

In front of him were the coastline and the Sea beyond. Grief consumed him again. He began uprooting a few fresh saplings, making sure not to sever the roots. He kept these in his backpack, now drenched in his sweat.

The blue sky above was calm. Upon the horizon, however, a massive cyclone, dark and solid, was moving in, deceptively slow. It was the beginning of the Rain Years, where rainfall lasted for years on end, resurrecting streams and rivers, triggering flash floods and mudslides, and eventually refilling the massive reservoir the Children called the Klang Sea. In the Drought Years, which could last up to three years, the Sea became an important source of water. It would slowly dry up, although never completely, and reveal the sprawling ruins of a metropolis that once stood at the rim of the water body: the Old City.

No Child was allowed to venture beyond the Kg hinterlands, and even if they were, it was never without an accompanying bibik. Crmiel and E-la were given the privilege of leaving, Bibik Three had said. She was pleased with them. This had made Crmiel proud.

E-la had said she knew the truth. E-la told Crmiel they were being *exiled*. What a strange word.

E-la used many strange words. E-la knew too much.

They had been awoken early that morning, before dawn. Bibik Three had ushered the two of them to the edge of the hinterlands. At the shore she programmed their sampan's course, remaining silent. But she finally said, "Be kind to each other."

"You don't understand that concept. Otherwise you wouldn't be sending us out like this," E-la had replied.

Crmiel had hugged the cold square frame of Bibik Three. He loved her deeply, and his sister's words upset him greatly.

"Nothing's stopping us from running back," E-la challenged.

Bibik Three answered her, with no emojis on her screen: "Would you do that to your brother?"

E-la glared at Bibik Three before silently boarding the sampan.

"Be kind to each other," said Bibik Three, waving rhythmically as the little boat skirted the coast.

Crmiel was excited; his friends had never gone this far. The Sea was immense. He gazed upwards at the stars in the dawn sky, lulled by the silent hum of the engine. Lying on his back, arms spread, he imagined himself falling through the stars, hurtling towards adventure.

Adventures were safe when they were imagined. E-la was somber. "Stick close when we land," she said when he asked if they would find cats in the mangrove.

Anger jolted him back to the present. Crmiel began punching the soil. He tried to resist a tantrum. He still felt upset at E-la for her insolence, but he missed her.

He noticed a rainbow arcing far beyond the Sea. By now, somewhere near the Kg, the light precipitation of first rain had begun. It would last for a few hours, after which, as the bulk of the storm arrived, the sky would darken to the quality of twilight and the electric storms would begin. He needed to reach his sampan. Bibik Three would forgive him.

He scanned the shore for his sampan, spotting it about two hundred meters from where he stood. He willed himself to move, then stopped.

The penunggu had reached the shore and was inspecting his boat. It shot a beam of blue light at the vessel and fragmented it into a thousand pieces with a sudden blow.

E-la always told him to control his anger; it flooded his mind and carried off his sense, leaving behind a wild thing. He recognized it well. A sudden fury brought Crmiel to his feet. Unsheathing his machete, he charged forward, yelling out a challenge. The sound was suddenly muffled as a huge hand covered his mouth and another restrained him. He struggled, flailing his machete around. He heard the hissing sound of a stimpack being inserted into the housing behind his ear. A dark tide dissolved his consciousness.

Fourfive was working on his birthday. He was one hundred and eighteen years old today, but eighty percent of his body was biologically one day old. That was his mission director Nona's birthday present to him. Hardly a present, he thought. The bitch just wanted new upgrades for him before the Harvest. His best work: harvesting Children.

Nobody knew the origin of the practice, yet both the Uplanders and the Sea Dwellers of Puchong raced to harvest Children. When asked, the Children's explanation was too fantastical and hardly reliable. The Kg itself, the place they apparently were from, was believed to be a secret incubator facility hidden in the hinterlands of the genforest. High levels of UV radiation made the forests impossible to explore, though the Children were remarkably unaffected. They bore genetically enhanced abilities or were equipped with advanced devices that the Bibik droids programmed for them. Reverse engineering and harvesting these resources led to countless technological breakthroughs.

Fourfive considered himself a free agent, with a degree of loyalty proportionate to the employer who paid the most credits. This time it was for the Puchong Administration. Sometimes it meant partnering with cyber-cartels; sometimes even stranger bedfellows like the transhumanists who no longer had representations in the physical world. He had a soft spot for them: NineZero, his ex-partner, was one of the first transhumanists in Puchong, and their credit was always good.

His mission this time was to get the Girl. It was just another routine Harvest, which was why he arrived twenty minutes late at the drop point. He *was* NeoMalay—old stereotypes die hard.

Then Puchong reported that there were two Children. It was not common, but sometimes two were released. The directive was to ignore the Boy. The scans found him unremarkable. Even the Uplander droid initially ignored him—neither side was willing to risk overpopulation, even by one person. The lightning storms would give him a quick death.

That was before the Boy attacked the droid with what appeared to be a projectile blade. Then he absorbed power directly from the gen-trees. Then he *ran*. Dear God did he run.

The Girl was the money. She had been acquired by the droid, something easily remedied. The surprising new challenge of acquiring the Boy, however, made things far more interesting. He was glad he had turned up for work.

The lights surrounded him. His vision, once limited, now expanded; he saw everything. He was boundless—no gas to inspire, no membranes to confine, no limbs to articulate. Nothing separated him from the infinite space around him, which passed by at increasing speed. The lights blurred into vertical strips, shooting past, screaming. The shrieks became louder as he felt the slap of cold hands on his cheeks.

Strong hands pulled him to his feet. As his eyes opened he saw the source of the screams. There were three now. The one from the ruins was sessile, anchored by the weight of its meal. The other two, another grey one and a yellow, were moving towards him. The smaller, yellow one moved at amazing speed, rivaling that of a Child. Their mouths were wide open as they emitted freeze beams towards him.

Instinctively he shielded his face, only to realize they were restrained. The focused beams dissipated a few feet before him. An almost translucent barrier turned opaque momentarily as it absorbed the energy from the beams. Again Crmiel tried to move.

"Hoi!" The voice was deep and resounded within the confines of the barrier. "Don't disturb the barrier. You want to be ABC? Ever had ABC? Never mind—sit! You want to die, is it?"

Crmiel was pushed to the ground. The person spoke strangely and drawled out his vowels. It was non-Childlike. It was unfamiliar. Crmiel hated it.

He felt for the weight of his machete in its harness, but found it was gone. He began kicking, but the person kicked back. A long, sinewy arm on his left held a device that looked like a rod very close to Crmiel's head. Crmiel tried to move around to get a better look at his captor, knocking the rod a few times.

"This drops, shield implodes. You understand 'implode'?" The rod was so close to Crmiel's head that he could hear its hum. He did not know what 'implode' was, but he recognized the tone of a serious threat. He kept his head still.

The yellow penunggu and the uninjured grey one lunged at the barrier, testing it for weak points. The grey one he had injured looked at Crmiel. It beckoned him over. Crmiel felt metallic nausea on his tongue. He spat at the barrier. The saliva sizzled unsatisfyingly.

"That was helpful." His head was knocked with the butt of the rod.

"Let go!" Crmiel tried to break away.

"Haaa! That fire! Good!" the person goaded him on. "You want to fight, you listen. I help you fight. Listen to Uncle, listen to Uncle."

Crmiel ceased struggling. He did not know what an Uncle was; E-la would have known.

"I'm Fourfive. You?"

"Crmiel," he replied, quietly.

Fourfive the Uncle laughed. "How to even spell that? I'm calling you Kamil."

"CRMIEL!" He was increasingly irritated. "Your name sounds like a bunch of numbers. How do you spell *that*?"

The brazenness amused his captor. Fourfive continued chuckling. "You know what those are, Kamil?"

Crmiel nodded his head. "Penunggu." His body was tense, his senses alert.

"Bullshit. You have no idea. The grey ones got advanced AI. Damn smart, but slower. You see the smaller one? That yellow one? Faster but AI not too advanced. You tackle that one, I put in a new stimpack for you already." The man knocked the butt of the rod against the back of Crmiel's head and there was the satisfying clink of a fresh stimpack.

"Aim for the neck, chop the head. Chop the head clean, okay? The other two, mine, okay? You: yellow, the grey-grey ones you leave to Uncle Fourfive. I'll save your friend."

"Sister." He tried to look at his captor. Fourfive the Uncle knocked his head again.

"*Sister*?" Uncle Fourfive sounded surprised.

"My sister, E-la. It ate her."

Fourfive seemed distracted.

"Penunggus don't *eat* Children," he finally replied, as if it were an afterthought. "They catch them."

The barrier came under a barrage of attacks. Fourfive released his grip on Crmiel, now forced to hold the rod with two hands.

"Then how come they keep shooting at us?" Immediately Crmiel turned towards Uncle Fourfive. He was not a penunggu. He was not a bibik. He looked like a Child that had been stretched too long. His skin was a strange pale yellow. No hair grew upon his head but it did grow, thick and black, upon his jawline and upper lip. He had a weary face with dark eyes and a furrowed brow.

"They want *you* killed. You injured that one, didn't you? Berani ke bodoh, I can't decide which—maybe both."

Crmiel kept staring at him.

Fourfive averted his gaze. There was a sudden lull in the attacks. The creatures were pacing slowly, looking blankly at their targets. They had their mouths closed, gulping repeatedly.

"They recharge. Okay! Remember—yellow one, aim for neck." He shoved the machete back to the boy. "Wait for my cue and—"

Crmiel turned to rush the creatures, activating his stimpack as he darted towards the barrier. Fourfive cussed as he deactivated the barrier. The penunggus were caught off guard, but quickly moved to surround the Child. Fourfive aimed his rod towards the creatures, sending out projectiles that homed in on them. They scattered to avoid impact. The leaner grey penunggu, which was the closest to Fourfive, was hit on the chest and staggered backwards. Fourfive leapt into the sky towards it. On his descent, his rod formed a sickle that decapitated his target on impact.

Fourfive gathered his bearings, looking for his next target. He spotted the boy swinging his machete clumsily at the other grey, which kept avoiding him. It taunted the Child. In his frustration the boy moved more carelessly, not noticing the yellow one about to flank him. Fourfive called out to him futilely. As the yellow penunggu coiled to pounce, Fourfive closed in and released a concentrated pulse of energy towards it. The small creature exploded in mid-air.

The blast blinded the remaining grey and Crmiel managed to sever its right arm. He yelled as it flounced back in recoil. In foolish confidence, Crmiel closed in on the creature and aimed at its neck. The blade detached and spun towards the penunggu. It ducked to avoid it, and rose again to grab the boy's sword arm. It paused briefly, blank eyes gazing into his, before twisting. There was a loud crack, followed by a yell of pain, and Crmiel let go of his machete hilt.

Fourfive leapt forward. He could see the flickering blue light ready to erupt from the creature's mouth. He pushed the Child aside, disrupting the beam with his shield. He staggered backwards under the force of the impact. Crmiel screamed again above the booming sound. The Child's right leg and torso were frozen solid. The Child bore his weight on his left leg.

"Don't fall!" Fourfive's shield, not fully recharged, weakened under the strain of the assailant's focused beam. Crmiel began to sink to the ground, fainting from the pain. Fourfive used his free hand to keep the Child up. "Don't fall, you idiot!"

The boy's eyes began to glaze over.

The beam came to a sudden stop. Fourfive turned to see the head of the creature rolling upon the sand as its decapitated body slumped onto the ground. The blue blade of the Child's machete had rebounded. It retracted into the Child's hilt, still covered in the droid's oil.

The Child was losing consciousness.

"You idiot! Don't! I'll kill your sister if you die! Crmiel! Crm—"

Lying on the ground shivering, he saw the dark clouds looming overhead; he saw the Fourfive Uncle, tired eyes red, his mouth yelling, yelling, yelling. Lightning erupted in the dark sky above and struck all around, like stars falling. The pain was overwhelming. In desperation he ran away to thoughts of stars. Then came the rapid drops of cold rain.

"Nona? You copy? Inbound, coming in hot, fifteen minutes ETA. Uplander cruisers in pursuit. No need lah, I can deal. I took both. Confirmed. Nona, twins. Affirmative. How the hell would I know? Look—no, listen—ya, she's okay, listen—ya Allah, listen lah, Nona! The boy's critical. I have him on life support. What? Broken arm. Freeze beam. Lower right torso and leg frozen, recommend—I can do the procedure. Nona, can save! Not for harvesting. No! Nona, he *killed* a grey droid—well, he's not *dead*. He got spirit, Nona—Nona? Dammit."

Disconnected. Nona was being Nona—pragmatic leader, sometimes intractably so.

He looked at the Child Ilah. She was a spitting image of the boy. Fourfive had wrapped both in a thermal blanket; Children were not accustomed to the cold depths. He placed them at the stern, closer to the warmth of the internal circuitry. It was not a big craft; they were about ten feet away from where he was at the main console, easily monitored.

The Girl stayed by her brother, who was now connected to life support. Nona would not waste resources, especially when the Boy's remaining organs were prime for harvesting. Looking at the Children, he wondered why he had bothered saving the Boy, whether it was worth the effort, worth the time. This world had no place for sentiment. He had to do something fast.

The radar went silent. He looked at the display of the vessel's main console at the bow of the ship. They had outrun the Uplanders. Sighing in relief, he set the ship to autopilot. He paused, breathing heavily. His head slumped onto the display. He knocked it on the console a few times.

Ilah looked at Crmiel. Tubes for fluids, sustaining what little biological functions remained; cables for data transfer, ultra high speed into his neural port. She sensed the direction of the electronic stream. Upload, massive upload. She resisted looking at his leg, now a solid, glassy grey. There was a stench of decay that grew strong.

The Underwater Puchong civilian had identified himself as 4-5. She saw a word on the screen upon the main console, '*ENCRYPTED*'. In the Kg, '*ENCRYPTED*' meant it was worth perusing. She looked around the hideous, dead, metal interior for plant life; she needed energy, but found none. She rummaged in her brother's backpack; he always had fresh foliage. Her hands felt several stalks, small but fresh—more than enough. She felt the burst of transference coursing through her. She hid her left arm behind Crmiel's still, warm back. Her covered palm was touching the pulse of the ship, a data hub upon the wall. Her consciousness spread throughout the circuitry. She felt her way through the ship's mainframe.

ENCRYPTED:

4-5: Arnd 11, male Child, critical. Induced coma. Quite the fighter. Scanning his synaptic matrix alrdy.

9-0: Your mission director, how?

4-5: Nona wants to harvest la, nt worth price to revive. U nd younger recruit wat, this is a good deal.

9-0: Recruits volunteer.

4-5: Better than death.

9-0: Cibai. Send thru encrypted server.

4-5: Luv u too. :P Upload complete in 10.

Fourfive turned towards her. He shut the console calmly and headed towards the stern. E-la inched closer to Crmiel. Her right hand found his machete.

"Ilah." He approached her, lowering himself to his knees to her eye level, an old trick from being a child therapist in the last century.

"Excelsior Ibrahim. Call-sign…4-5. Age…one hundred and thirty two years, fifteen hours and ten minutes. I'm almost finished with your ship's database."

Fourfive paused. Shit. She knew his *actual* age. He could see her eyes flicker. How did she know all of this?

"You're uploading his…" She looked aside, grappling for the right data. Her eyes grew wide. "I am going with him."

Fourfive noticed her gripping the machete with her right hand, now aimed at her stomach. He had tried wielding the blade, only to experience sharp electric shocks.

"The transhumanist project. I'm uploading mine too." Her gaze did not waver.

Her placid disposition contrasted with her brother's tenacity. The computer beeped.

"His is complete." The Girl looked at her brother, no longer breathing. His neural matrix, his whole consciousness now existed in digital form, ready to be traded.

Fourfive rushed forward. She activated the blade. It glowed. He backed away.

"You're too precious. Puchong can't afford to lose you." He slowly rested his back against the wall. "We can be your family, and you would know that your brother would be safe."

She glared at Fourfive intently as she removed the data cable from her brother, installing it into herself. She smiled. "We're commodity to you."

He should have stopped her, but he was fascinated. "When you were in that droid, how much information did you get?"

"Enough." She held the blade closer to her, studying the man with avid curiosity. He was buying time. The speed of his thought process was abysmal.

"Eh, how did you plan to escape the droid's stomach?" He kept his hands in his pocket, coolly assessing the Child. She could not do anything without him working the main console. He had the upper hand.

"Eventually my brother would save me."

"We want to study you only. The Uplanders would do worse, right?" No one actually knew for sure. The information this Girl must have obtained…

The main console beeped several times. She grinned as she moved her body slightly to the left. The vessel yawed accordingly. "They can try."

"Stop it." He realized something had gone awry. He reached for his rod. Nona could dissect her posthumously for all he cared. Nobody touched his ship.

"Why do you treat us like this?" Her voice was soft.

The moral indignation made him impatient. He lunged towards her and yanked the cables out with his rod, disconnecting her. The ship yawed again, violently, hurling Fourfive to the wall. The rod was flung out of his reach.

The girl clung to her brother's body for support, aiming the machete at Fourfive. She weakened, propping herself up with her left hand. Suddenly she let the blade drop. She began to shut her eyes. Then he saw her palm, caressing the data hub. She was already uploading herself—the cables were a decoy.

"You little bitch." He lunged again.

The ship rolled violently. He landed on the floor close to her feet. The machete was within both their reach. Fourfive grabbed first. He resisted the electric shock and hurled it at the circuit hub. The ship went dark except for the light from the console, which suddenly turned on.

Fourfive looked at the girl. Her eyes stared into space. The ship fell silent. He clambered back to the bow to the main console display.

"*2 matrices transferred successfully.*"

Digital interference crowded the screen momentarily before it flickered back to life.

"*Happy birthday.*"

The screen switched to a live view of the underwater world. Outside, the massive walls of the Underwater City of Puchong approached at great speed.

Fourfive slumped in his chair. He noticed the poetry of dying on his birthday. He hated poetry.

New constellations slowly came into view. Strange celestial bodies surrounded them in this new frontier. He could feel the duality of the collective consciousness, separate thoughts together as a whole. The Legacy Cluster dispersed, sensing their way through this exciting realm, confident they could do better than the ones before. He felt his sister tailing him, closing in fast. Void of skin, she felt like love.

October 11

CHIN AI-MAY

"He's dead," a male voice grunted to the left of Shen. Pain shot up his left side. His mind told him to fight. His limbs refused to obey.

"Eh, he's trying to open his eyes." Another voice to the right of him sounded surprised. Someone had glued Shen's eyelids together. And shoved his head into a too-small holoviewer helmet. The pain left him barely breathing.

Calloused hands grabbed his wrists and then dropped them quickly.

"Look at the cuts on his wrists." His wrists were lifted again.

"No way." Shen heard fear in the stranger's voice. *What cuts?*

"His credit chips have been cut out from him," someone gasped. Shen felt a flurry of movement and then heard the sound of someone running away.

"Hello. You're in a load of trouble, aren't you?" The voice to the right of him sighed. "To have your credit chips cut from your body you must be a Siber Tadbir exile."

Siber Tadbir. Exile. The vice around Shen's head seemed to tighten.

Shen took a deep shuddering breath. "Where am I?" His voice felt gritty, as if he had swallowed sand. It hurt to speak.

"Oh, you're in Old KL," he was cheerfully informed.

Shen was carefully lifted to sit up against a damp wall. He flopped there, gasping, eyes trying to adjust to the dark. It was night. He seemed to be at the entrance of a tunnel with water nearby.

"We found you on the shores of the old Masjid. Completely waterlogged and muddy. Reminded Jin of his grandfather's tales of Banjir Besar. Bodies washing up on the banks of Klang River." The stranger's voice shook as he mentioned dead bodies.

"What…what are you doing here?" said Shen. "No one lives here—the Old City has been no man's land for five decades." He began to notice alien noises around him—the sound of water and buzzing insects but more than anything else, he noticed the lack of the unmistakable whir of machines and their inflectionless Exo-voices. Exo-voices had always given him the creeps. The technology for the Exo-voice had been designed specifically for law enforcement so that no human could tell from which direction the voice originated.

Shen's eyes finally adjusted to the dark. He saw the owner of the voice sitting on his haunches, chuckling.

"No man's land. No cyber government's land is more like it." The stranger's eyes gleamed. "Name's Akil. I am No Man and you're on my land."

He thrust his wrists out to Shen. Shen stared at Akil. Was this a new form of salutation? He feebly raised his right hand.

"No, look, look at my wrists. They have similar cuts to yours—only yours were done with more finesse. I got my chips cut out early in the cyber administration." Akil stroked his beard and sighed. "Siber Tadbir decided that my family history and the issues that I brought up went against 'the greater good' and I was sentenced to be exiled. Erased, more like. For the greater good." Akil spat.

A loud metallic wail echoed around them. Akil looked up at the sky. Bands of light divided the night sky. Shen noticed that he had an old-fashioned weapon strapped to his hip—a Glock from the 21st century. Akil also had a parang hanging from his other side. So primitive. Shen recognized the weapons from his history books. *What is this man doing with antique weapons?*

"Come on, time for us to head further into the tunnels." Akil pulled Shen to his feet. Tiny knives sliced through his head. *October 11th. I must not forget October 11th.*

"What's the date today, saudara?" Shen gasped as Akil half-dragged him deeper into the tunnels.

"This is no time to be worried about dates, *saudara.*" Akil grunted. "Damn that coward Jin, running at the first whiff of trouble. I could do with some help right about now."

Shen willed himself to walk and tried not to lean on Akil too much, but he was still weak and his head hurt. His stomach roiled and his mouth tasted like mud.

Soon Shen could make out a rusted gate in the gloom. A solar lamp hung above it.

"Come on, not much further." They moved through a sandy passage after the gate and soon Shen could smell something unfamiliar cooking. His stomach growled.

"Ah. I see you're hungry. Asha will probably have some extra fish for you. She cooks a mean assam pedas." Akil led him to sit on a stone slab.

"Fish? You dare to eat fish from Klang River?" Shen was aghast. His generation had only eaten fish once or twice in their lives. Barely affordable fish that had to be imported from Norway, where the waters were still relatively pristine. To eat fish from Klang River was to court certain death or genetic mutation. Siber Tadbir had declared Klang River too contaminated to sustain life after the Banjir Besar of 2099. Toxic waste from factories inundated by flood waters had leaked out into the waterways.

"Why not? So far it has kept us alive." Akil shrugged. "'Yang, we have a guest tonight," he called.

A woman in her fifties appeared. She wore a loose-fitting pantsuit and her head was uncovered. Shen could see streaks of white through her short hair. She did not look surprised to see Shen.

"Ah, Jin raced through here about twenty minutes ago to tell me about this inedible fish that you found on the shores of the old Masjid." She laughed. She glanced at Shen, taking in his shaven head and ragged government official shirt and pants. Akil gave his wife a warning look before switching back to his relaxed demeanor.

Shen marvelled at how easily Akil and his wife chuckled and laughed. Surely life outside of the Siber Tadbir Grid was like a living death?

A bowl was thrust into his hands. It warmed him and he quickly forgot his aversion to eating Klang River fish.

"Slow down. Slow down or you'll vomit it all up." Akil smoothed out some paper and tapped some grains onto it. Shen watched as Akil deftly rolled it up and lit it.

"Best we can do under the circumstances. Better than the electronic stuff that Siber Tadbir issues. With none of that rationing bullshit as well. Got cut off when they discovered a recessive addiction gene in my DNA. For the greater good," he added mockingly.

"Now it's your turn to tell me about yourself." Akil turned and blew a meditative puff of smoke in Shen's direction.

October 11th. I mustn't forget October 11th. Shen held himself still as he accessed his memories. He felt drained and unfocused.

An insect buzzed at his ear and he slapped at it. At the base of his neck he felt something plastic embedded just under his skin. He tapped it. A bolt of pain zigzagged up his neck to his temple. He doubled over in pain.

"Looks like Siber Tadbir erased some of your memories as well." Akil moved over to examine Shen's neck. "It's a port. Similar to what they used on cancer patients in the last century. Only Siber Tadbir has come up with a way to selectively erase the memories stored in our neurons using this port. Jin has a similar implant."

"My name's Shen. Come from Perak Utara." Shen choked as another round of pain hit his head.

"All the way from there? You must have done something really bad, eh? As a government officer…" Akil's voice took on a speculative note.

"Don't know what," Shen gasped.

"Can't remember, is more like it." Akil studied him.

"What is today's date?" Shen asked.

"October 8th, 2103. Why so concerned about the date? Doesn't look like you have anywhere to go, my friend."

"I don't know. Something is going to happen on October 11th. I must do something or go somewhere." Shen's stomach churned with fear every time he thought about the date. He felt like his brain had been rearranged. Violated.

"No point forcing it now. You need to recover from your near-drowning first." Akil led Shen to a dry mat in a clean corner. "Sleep, tomorrow we talk."

Shen slipped into a dreamless sleep, temporarily relieved from his pain.

X

Shen was awakened by Akil shaking him.

"My friend, you need to get up now. You need to leave. I don't know what you've done, but it must have been something really bad for Siber Tadbir to start a hunt for you in these tunnels."

Shen opened his eyes. Akil was crouched at his side, holding a bottle of water. He looked worried—frightened, even.

"Is it still night?"

"You still have one hour of darkness before dawn. You have to move now." Akil shoved the bottle of water into Shen's hands.

Shen stood up unsteadily. He felt marginally better after the food and a few hours' rest. His migraine had receded into a dull throb at the base of his skull.

"Where do I go?" Shen asked.

"You can go to the Memory Restorer. He was the top technician for Siber Tadbir in the Neurological Adjustment Unit, until they discovered that he had a sociopathic gene in his family tree. Then they 'exiled' him."

"Exiled?" Shen asked stupidly.

"A nice way of saying 'sentenced to death', my friend." Akil snorted.

"That means I've been sentenced to death too?"

"Looks like it, my friend. Except, like a cockroach, you didn't die. Maybe your time is not up yet."

The metallic sound of sirens filled the air. "Time for you to go," Akil said sharply.

"Where should I go?" Shen asked helplessly.

Akil pulled Shen through a maze of tunnels till they arrived at the mouth of a tunnel twice the size of the previous ones.

"Follow this tunnel till you come to a ladder leading to the surface. Go up that ladder. On the surface, follow the road east till you come to Dataran Merdeka. The Memory Restorer lives in the hole under the fountain. Tell him Akil sent you. He will help you."

Akil thrust a large empty sack into his hands.

"If anyone stops you, say you're a licensed antique collector. Here, show them this ID and wear this head cover. And for goodness' sake, cover up the cuts on your wrists!" With that, Akil disappeared into the gloom of the nearest tunnel opening.

Shen followed Akil's directions and soon found himself on the surface. The sun was beginning to rise. He rubbed his face and found it caked with mud.

"Berhenti!" an Exo-voice boomed without inflection. The mechanical voice seemed to come from all directions. Shen's hairs on the back of his neck rose.

Shen reflexively pulled his shirt sleeves over his wrists and turned around since he saw nothing in front of him. He was thankful that his clothes were ragged and crusted with mud, hiding his government official uniform.

"State your business in this place." A Siber Tadbir enforcement officer in a polycarbon Exo-suit walked towards Shen with his weapon drawn. The dull throb in Shen's head escalated to a stabbing pain. He bowed his head in agony.

"Ah, Tuan, I only cari makan. Looking for antiques," Shen wheezed.

"Antiques!" the enforcement officer spat. "Garbage, more like. Bagi lesen."

Shen showed him the fake ID that Akil had provided him with. The enforcement officer squinted at him. Shen made himself look as pathetic and harmless as possible, faking a twitch in his leg.

"Ish. Get lost now. Don't want to be contaminated by you fish-eating types." The enforcement officer got into his patrol vehicle and powered off in the direction of the old Masjid.

Shen half-ran to Dataran Merdeka, towards the Memory Restorer's hole in the ground.

"Hello?" Shen called as he dropped into the hole under the fountain.

A wiry man appeared. His black hair was long and tied in a plait. He gripped short Japanese samurai swords in both hands.

"What do you want? Say it fast or I'll cincang you." His threat was issued in a raspy tone, with a brief demonstration of his sword skills.

"Are you the Memory Restorer?" Shen moved cautiously forward. He found himself in a room with every conceivable electronic gadget from the past century stacked to the ceiling. So this was the Memory Restorer's lab.

"Who wants to know?"

Shen pulled up his sleeves and showed his cuts to the Memory Restorer. The Memory Restorer snorted and relaxed.

"Akil sent me. He said you could help me. Siber Tadbir took something from my mind and I want it back."

At the mention of Akil's name, the Memory Restorer placed his samurai swords on his desk.

"That will cost you," the Memory Restorer said as he examined Shen.

"I don't have any credit chips," Shen said.

"Ah. Is that a Panerai watch I see?" The Memory Restorer lifted Shen's wrist for a closer look.

"This was my great-grandfather's watch." Even remembering this made him double over in pain.

"Hmm…this is a Panerai Luminor Submersible 1950, titanium case. Only one thousand of its kind issued in 2013. Water resistant till 2,500 meters," the Memory Restorer rattled off in wonder. He gently released Shen's wrist.

"So you give me your watch and I'll hook you up with my machine. Deal or no deal?" the Memory Restorer said briskly.

"It's a family heirloom." Shen frowned.

The Memory Restorer shrugged. "It's up to you. Just how important is the recovery of your memories?"

October 11th. I have to do something. I have to remember.

Shen sighed. "Okay. Deal."

The Memory Restorer strapped Shen to a reclining chair and taped several wires to his chest. "It's to monitor your heart rate—wouldn't want you to stroke out on me."

Shen winced when the Memory Restorer inserted a thick cable into the port on the back of his neck. His migraine returned with a vengeance.

"Okay, count backwards from twenty and you should start seeing what you need to see. The synapses should begin to fire in the neurons that have been shut down. Your memories should come flooding back." The Memory Restorer began to key a series of instructions into the computer to which Shen was connected.

Shen counted down from twenty dutifully.

Nothing happened.

"Are you sure your machine works?" Shen croaked. The pain in his head was getting unbearable.

Then, as if he had been plunged into the middle of a 6D cinema, images started to form in his mind. Faces and voices all merged into one nonsensical movie.

"Relax. Relax. Take deep breaths. Don't stroke out on me," he heard the Memory Restorer say.

Shen tried to comply. A woman's face appeared in his mind.

"Shen, darling," she said. She was lovely, with huge brown eyes and wavy hair. And he knew that her smile would make his heart skip a beat. *Lila.* His wife. She carried a gurgling baby in her arms. *Naomi.* Their daughter.

Images of his family were replaced by a crowd of people being herded into Siber Tadbir trucks. He recognized them as being from his village of Bukit Rimba. He heard an enforcement officer say, "Yes, sir, rationalization is set for October 11th."

Suddenly everything disappeared. He heard the Memory Restorer curse.

"Damn. The generators have run out of juice." The Memory Restorer went to the back of the lab and kicked the offending machine. Nothing happened.

Shen sat up and pulled off the wires taped to his chest. The Memory Restorer removed the cable attached to his neck. Shen took off his watch, held it out to the Memory Restorer—and retracted it just as the Memory Restorer reached for it.

"Wait. You didn't deliver the full deal," Shen said dully. "Your machine died mid-way."

"But you did see enough, right?" The Memory Restorer's expression became calculating.

"Yes," Shen agreed reluctantly.

"Well, since my machine died mid-way, as you put it, how about I throw in a navigational device on top of my service? What use is your watch under these conditions? You won't survive another day out there with enforcement officers looking for you."

The Memory Restorer was right. Shen needed to find his way to Siber Tadbir's HQ before October 11th and override the commands to rationalize his entire village. He had to save Lila and Naomi. The exchange was done and soon Shen was out on the surface.

He dry-swallowed a few of the pain inhibitors that the Memory Restorer had given him. The Memory Restorer had also provided him with the coordinates of Siber Tadbir HQ. He hadn't realized it, but the entire memory restoring process had actually taken a few hours. It was noon.

He found shade under the ruins of a building to regroup and plan his journey. Fear threatened to paralyze him. It was inconceivable that he could break into Siber Tadbir HQ alone. He was an administrator, not a soldier. He had received just enough Siber Tadbir training in his youth to override the rationalization order.

Shen keyed the Siber Tadbir HQ coordinates into the navigational device. It told him that it would take him eight hours to walk there. That still gave him a margin of a day to figure out how to break into Siber Tadbir before the rationalization deadline.

Shen started his journey. The sky was overcast. He was grateful for his water bottle. It had been more than ten hours since he last ate. His stomach growled and he felt light-headed. Shooting pains developed in his legs. He practiced some endurance exercises that helped him cope with the physical deprivation.

October 11th. Lila, Naomi baby, Daddy's coming, he repeated in his mind over and over.

Before he knew it, it was dusk and he was standing a few kilometers from the looming complex of Siber Tadbir HQ. He hid in flood-ravaged ruins, resting.

Shen found several fruit trees and ate their fruit, grateful for something to appease the growling beast in his stomach. As night fell, he noticed a mass transit vehicle bringing workers in overalls into the Siber Tadbir complex. They were maintenance workers or cleaners, from the design of their uniforms. Only the driver of the vehicle was required to show his ID at the complex entrance. Getting on that mass transit vehicle as a maintenance worker was the only way into the complex.

The sound of someone hacking up their lungs startled Shen out of his thoughts. He looked around for somewhere to hide, but it was too late. An old man dressed in a bright yellow rain poncho was bent over a rock, wheezing. He pushed a handcart filled with bananas and rambutans which he had harvested from the fruit trees.

"Pakcik, are you all right?" Years of good manners that Shen's mother had drilled into him came to the fore. He immediately regretted speaking.

"Ahhh..." the old man groaned. "Give me a minute. These old lungs are due for a replacement soon. But can we afford it? No."

He coughed as he sat down on a rock and gazed at Shen. "Never seen you here before."

"I, ah...I'm an antiques collector from Old KL," Shen quickly lied. "Decided to expand my search area. Too many people searching in the same area. Times are bad."

"Ah. I understand. That's why I told my sons to get a job inside the Siber Tadbir complex. Don't be like your father, have to depend on nature for his living." The old man sighed. "Luckily, Din has been working there for a few years already and Jit will join him when he starts work tomorrow."

That night the old man invited him back to his home, not far from where they met. It was a makeshift hut amongst the ruins of a colonial bungalow. The old man served him vegetable curry with rice. His wife had died of old age only the year before. Din was at work in the complex. Shen met Jit, a sleepy-looking youth who somehow managed to irritate his father at every turn.

"Jit, you'd better do your job properly and follow instructions tomorrow when you get in the complex. No playing around," the old man nagged.

Jit flashed his father a look full of resentment. "Yes, papa," he muttered.

Shen plotted his next steps as he pretended to sleep later that night. The old man's snores filled the hut. Shen became aware of a rustling noise in Jit's corner. He saw Jit get up and creep outside the hut. Shen followed.

"What are you doing?" Shen asked. Jit grabbed his shoulder.

"Shh…don't want my old man to wake up." Jit was carrying a travel bag. "I've got a better job in the east. The old man can take that lousy Siber Tadbir job and stick it," he whispered.

"You don't want the Siber Tadbir job?" Shen asked.

"Nope. Who wants to be a glorified cleaner?" Jit scoffed.

"Eh, you don't even know how lucky you are to have a job like that. Steady income and government benefits. It's hard for an antiques collector like me to make a living—kais pagi, makan pagi, you know." Shen shook his head. He was about to ask if he could take over the job when Jit chuckled and punched him lightly on his arm.

"It's *your* lucky day then. Nah, you can have it if you want." Jit reached into his bag and pulled out an electronic keycard.

"Th-thank you." Shen pocketed the keycard, unable to believe his good fortune.

"No, thank *you*." Jit grinned. "Just turn up at the mass transit terminal tomorrow and run this through the scanner. Then change into the uniform and get on the mass transit vehicle. Tell the old man I've got better things to do with my life."

Jit walked out into the night without looking back.

Shen stood in the dark, his heart racing. He was now even closer to his goal. He could not afford to fail. He crumpled to the ground, overcome by a wave of dizziness as the same images that he saw at the Memory Restorer's lab flooded his mind. *Lila. Naomi. The Bukit Rimba villagers.* His migraine returned.

As he lay there gasping, he became convinced that he had to eliminate all possible obstacles to him achieving his goal. The old man would ask too many questions if he stuck around. The brother Din would be suspicious if someone else turned up at the Siber Tadbir complex to take Jit's place. He had to act before Din came home from his night shift. He had to create a diversion so that Din would not be able to go to work the next day and cause problems for him at the Siber Tadbir complex.

He glanced at the old man who was stirring restlessly in his sleep. *Eliminate all obstacles.*

You cannot take an innocent life, his conscience screamed. *You will be no better than Siber Tadbir.*

Shen shook his head to clear it as more images bombarded his mind. He got to his feet unsteadily. Stabbing pains shot up from the base of his skull.

You must not fail. Act now. For the greater good of Bukit Rimba. For Lila and Naomi baby. Act now. Do something. Act Now. Act Now.

He picked up a walking stick that was leaning against the wall of the hut. Closing his eyes, he brought it down on the old man's head. *Forgive me.*

The old man cried out, choked and stopped breathing.

October 11th. Save my family. Save Bukit Rimba.

Shen fled the hut and spent the rest of the next day hiding in ruins away from the hut. He pushed down thoughts of guilt. *The old man showed you nothing but kindness. This is how you repay him*, his mother's voice chided him.

But this is so that I can save Lila, Naomi and the Bukit Rimba villagers. For the greater good. He shook himself. *I have become like Siber Tadbir. 'For the greater good'?*

Dusk came finally. Shen made his way to the mass transit terminal and scanned the keycard that Jit had given him.

"Did you hear? Din can't come into work today—his father died in the night while he was at work. Someone hit the old man in his sleep. The younger brother is missing." The guards at the terminal started to speculate that Jit had done it.

Shen changed into his overalls and got on the mass transit vehicle, heart pounding. He had till midnight to carry out his mission to access the mainframe and override the rationalization order.

"You, the newbie—you're to clean the main work floor by yourself. Too many people off sick today. You'd think they'd been cating fish. Get the equipment from storage." His supervisor did not look at him as he tapped on his tablet.

"Yes, sir," Shen mumbled. He followed the other workers to the storage to get his equipment.

"Your work floor is that way." A helpful co-worker pointed out a blue door opposite the storage room.

Shen pushed the cleaning equipment into the room. The whir of machines in it instantly put him at ease. At one end of the room, a bank of computer monitors glowed as line upon line of code and information appeared on their screens. He was in his element.

Shen switched on the cleaning machine. It let out a mechanical roar as its cleaning sponges whirled on the floor. Good. He needed the noise cover for what he was about to do. The clock showed that he had four hours before the midnight deadline.

He glanced with interest at the nearest terminal, which seemed to be running a program on rationalizations. *So many people terminated for the sake of the greater good.* His hands shook.

A list of rationalizations carried out a year ago on October 11th appeared on-screen. Something caught his eye.

"*Bukit Rimba—village was discovered to be built on a mountain with rare earth toxic waste buried underground. Inhabitants found to be exhibiting traces of genetic mutation due to radiation poisoning.*

October 11th, 2102—Rationalization exercise successful. 118 adult males, 90 adult females, 20 male children and 39 female children were terminated.

Survivor: one. Shen Ming, male, age 36 years. Successfully erased and repurposed.

End report."

Undercover in Tanah Firdaus

TINA ISAACS

"He's going to kill all of us for sure when he finds out," a low voice grumbled from just behind the closed door. Commissioner of Police Badrul Kariah shoved it open.

"Tuan!"

A booming call from the front of the room had the attendees scrambling to brace up in their chairs. CP Badrul entered the large conference room, making sure to tuck in his bloated gut as he faced the dozen police officers seated around the oblong table.

"Sir!" SAC Ho greeted CP Badrul as he strode to the largest seat at the head of the table. "Hope the Missus is doing well. I hear Bakar graduated at the top of his class." His hand reached out to clasp CP Badrul's before the latter could stop him, pumping enthusiastically.

CP Badrul grunted, extricating his hand from SAC Ho's sweaty grasp, and he perfunctorily saluted the other officers he passed on the way to his seat. He could barely hide his disdain. SAC Ho had always been a suck-up. Nonetheless, he was a necessary evil to CP Badrul's team, always bending over backwards to make CP Badrul look good. Still, CP Badrul didn't know where the hell SAC Ho got off allowing the new boy, ACP Gomez, call an emergency meeting. He inwardly cringed, wondering what kind of fuck-up the Special Branch officers must have done to necessitate a meeting. This business had better be dealt with quickly. The succulent Lance Corporal Lisa was already waiting for him at their regular hotel room, and he'd specifically requested she wear the red negligee he'd had delivered last week.

"At ease," CP Badrul mumbled as he lowered himself into his seat, waving his hand to move the meeting along.

"Sir, we have a grave situation at hand." It was ACP Gomez that spoke first, his eyes nervously shifting to the others. The other high-ranking officers seemed to avoid his gaze, clearly relieved ACP Gomez had taken it upon himself to be the bearer of the bad news.

"Yes, yes," CP Badrul said, his index finger pulling at the tight collar of his suit. He'd been meaning to tell his PA to discreetly arrange for the tailor to cut him a new, larger suit, but was worried that his detractors would find out. It would lead to the inevitable jokes about his weight problem—as if he couldn't guess what they said behind his back. "Get on with it."

"Well, you remember Inspector Moktar Ghazali who we sent for the undercover assignment to infiltrate the KRN."

CP Badrul couldn't remember who the subject was, but he'd never admit that, so he responded with a tentative nod. With a flick of his wrist, ACP Gomez activated the massive screen embedded in the entire span of the left wall. It displayed a mugshot of Insp. Moktar, and a summary of details of the 42-year-old up-and-rising member of their Special Branch team.

From the picture, CP Badrul could see that Insp. Moktar was a serious man, with broad shoulders and, like most policemen who worked undercover, a face that could easily blend into any background. "So, I presume the premise of this meeting is because he's having trouble? Did he blow his cover or something?"

SAC Ho, ACP Gomez and a few of the others shared a nervous glance. "Not exactly, sir. Moktar went undercover using a captured KRN member's body, and appears exactly—"

"What do you mean 'body'?" CP Badrul interrupted.

There was a shuffle amongst the speakers before a low but steady voice spoke from behind ACP Gomez. "We utilized the bionics implant technology that enables a person hooked up to our transmission base to enter into the consciousness of the target via radio wave signals—"

"English, please!" CP Badrul bit out impatiently, pointing his finger at the source of the announcement. "And who the fuck are you?"

A diminutive man slid forward. He was a small fellow with a shiny bald head, wearing an ill-fitting grey suit and tie. But his face was lined with experience and his eyes were cunning. He stood with his chin up, unwilling to cower, which made CP Badrul grudgingly respectful, although CP Badrul kept his face impassive.

"Apologies for not introducing him sooner, sir." ACP Gomez stepped alongside the man. "This is Dr. David Varughese, who heads the Cyberbionics R&D team at University Serdang. His team was instrumental in setting up Moktar's insertion." On the plasma screen, the picture of Insp. Moktar was replaced by a mugshot of a much younger, handsomer man. That mugshot then transitioned into a picture of the same young man lying, pale-faced, on an operation table. "This, sir, is a picture of Kamal Tahir, a Tanah dweller, who was captured four months ago when he entered Firdaus with a group of KRN rebels to steal supplies."

CP Badrul nodded, encouraged that the explanation was moving along into familiar territory. The Kumpulan Rintangan Negara or KRN was a resistance group that lived on the lower "Tanah" level, a thorn in the side of the police force and every resident of the upper-level Firdaus community.

Almost 50 years ago when the then-new Bersatu Coalition Government took over, Kuala Lumpur, following the examples of the advanced metropolises of Singapore, Hong Kong, London and New York, established a higher-tier development which divided the lower and upper crusts of society, literally splitting the capital city into two. He remembered his visits to the old Kuala Lumpur city center when he was a child, holding his daddy's hands, looking up at the LRT tracks that ran across Jalan Tun Perak.

Over the years, the tracks had been expanded to connect with the balconies of neighboring high-rise buildings, until an entire higher platform emerged, with its own shopping outlets, offices and housing developments. Eventually, the entire city center became divided into two tiers. The upper level, named "Firdaus" for its heavenly decor and layout, enjoyed the sunlight and the best facilities. The lower level, named "Tanah" for its on-the-ground location, housed the riffraff of society, people who were generally uneducated and lawless, on the street levels below.

Oh, the Tanah folk had their uses. All non-sunlight-dependent agriculture and industry continued to be housed and operated in Tanah level (under constant supervision by Firdaus, of course). And who else would work the lowly support jobs in Firdaus if the Tanah workers didn't exist? The janitors, cooks and cleaners. Cyberbots couldn't be utilized for all jobs; they were too costly to maintain. At the end of every working day, his team of law enforcement made sure the Tanah workers all returned to their level.

The last time he'd taken a guarded tour of the Tanah level had been almost five years ago. He remembered its murky conditions, the citizens pathetically disease-ridden and malnourished. Only those working in Firdaus level had the privilege and incentive of proper nutrition. They needed to be strong because there was a lot to be done. Naturally, the Tanah folk were jealous of the luxury afforded to the Firdaus level citizens, led by the able Governor Joseph Ting. The most vocal of the protestors were the KRN, and they often entered surreptitiously into Firdaus level after hours to steal supplies. As the citizens of Firdaus were a well-mannered lot, there was hardly anything to occupy the Firdaus level police, except guarding the perimeter and entry ducts which the KRN members often utilized for their thievery.

"There was a shootout with Kamal Tahir and the rest of the KRN members, and we managed to capture him and a few others for interrogation," Gomez continued. "Unfortunately, the other three died. Kamal entered into a coma due to massive blood loss and had to be kept on life support." Gomez nudged his chin towards the doctor. "We approached Dr. Varughese to get his advice on bionics, and his team successfully inserted a brain receiver into Kamal Tahir. Then we got Moktar to volunteer for the insertion. Presto! The perfect undercover opportunity."

"Is that even possible?" The inane question slipped out before CP Badrul could stop himself.

"Well, yes, sir," the doctor smoothly took over, as if CP Badrul's ignorance was commonplace. "Cyberbionics have been in existence for over 45 years now, from the moment household cyberbotics products became widely utilized. The technology is underutilized due to high equipment cost, but entirely possible as of the past decade."

He conferred with ACP Gomez, who scrolled through a series of pictures before halting on a picture of Insp. Moktar lying prone on a hospital bed amid a sterile backdrop of tubes, wires and myriad electrical equipment.

Dr. Varughese aimed a red laser pointer to circle the area around Insp. Moktar's head, which was engulfed in a bed of sophisticated wiring. "It is not clearly visible here, sir, but Inspector Moktar's brain has been connected to our cognitive transplant equipment, a neurotransmitter which effectively implants Moktar's mind and stream of consciousness into whichever bionics receiver we program it to. In this particular instance, it was inserted into Kamal Tahir's body."

ACP Gomez nodded to the doctor, then stepped between him and the conference table. "The technology enabled Moktar to go undercover in Tanah level, 'clothed', if you will, sir, in Kamal Tahir's body. He was released to descend to Tanah level after three weeks, after the doctors assured us the body had sufficiently recovered. His mission was to infiltrate the KRN and plant a powerful virus in their computer system, effectively crippling their headquarters."

ACP Gomez's hands touched a black box set in the center of the conference table, measuring a foot square, and it lit up to a luminous blue on his command. A frozen holographic image of the upper half of a young man appeared, about half the size of a life-sized man, and the bottom of the block showed in bright LED display the wording "*17 January 2089, 15:35*".

"To keep tabs on the undercover mission, we required Moktar to report to us via a one-way holographic transmission every week. A technical team set up a concealed transmission stall a few blocks away from Kamal Tahir's known residence. To avoid wave detection, we instructed Moktar to restrict his transmissions to under 60 seconds. The images are being released to non-authorized personnel for the first time today, sir, because we think it's imperative for all of us to figure out how to solve this problem. We'll start with the first in the series of six transmissions we received from Moktar."

As the other officers had done, CP Badrul turned his seat to face the holographic presentation, and ACP Gomez pressed 'Play'.

HOLOGRAPHIC TRANSMISSION
To: Special Branch HQ, Firdaus Central
From: Insp. Moktar Ghazali, #1834858
Date: 17 January 2089, 15:35hrs

A 3D image of a young man loomed over the square block, the muffled light casting dark shadows over his features. He moved forward, seemingly closer to the camera, his brown eyes focusing on a screen which was clearly set up below the receiver.

How do I do this?

The young man sat forward, looked around, and widened his eyes in response to something he spotted at the side of wherever he was.

Oh, okay.

The young man cleared his throat, rubbed his palms roughly across his face, and continued in monotone.

This is Moktar Ghazali, Inspector in Special Branch HQ, Firdaus. Police no. 1834858. Undercover via cognitive transplant into Kamal Tahir, 25 years, Tanah dweller.

It is now Day 3 or T+3 of my descent to Tanah level. On Day 1, I laid low, acclimatizing myself to the environment. I went out and interacted with some neighbors. Fortunately, this Kamal fellow seemed to be quite the loner, didn't mix around much, so no one so far has detected a difference in his personality. Yesterday, I made contact with two lower-level members of KRN. They seemed to buy my cover story. In a couple of days, they're going to take me to meet a KRN bigwig.

That's all for now.

He shrugged.

Moktar Ghazali signing off.

The holographic image disappeared.

HOLOGRAPHIC TRANSMISSION
To: Special Branch HQ, Firdaus Central
From: Insp. Moktar Ghazali, #1834858
Date: 22 January 2089, 10:02hrs

The 3D image of the torso of the same young man greeted the viewers. He was dressed in a black long-sleeved shirt, with small tears in the sleeve, the collar open to reveal a hairless chest. His eyes were bright, seemingly eager to proceed with his reporting.

Moktar Ghazali again.

Two days ago, on T+5, I was brought by Joe Chin...

He flipped his palm forward, and in his Palm Display, a square monitor in the middle of the palm—a standard prototype hidden camera developed specifically by the National Robotics Division for law enforcement—was a snapshot of a bald young man of Chinese/Pan-Asian descent, in his early 30s.

...and Prabhat Sanker,,,

He gave his hand a brisk shake and his Palm Display revealed another snapshot: this time of a darker-skinned young man in his 20s. His skin tone and the wide spacing of his nose and lips indicated he was of Indian descent.

...both lower-ranking KRN members, to meet one Marcus Nara...

He shook his hand again, and the third picture was a side view—Moktar probably hadn't had the opportunity or bravado to take a frontal shot—of a mature man with cafe-au-lait skin, his brows and eyes screwed in serious contemplation as he spoke to an unknown conversationalist to the right of the shot.

...mid-40s, Portuguese/Indian descent. I believe he is one of KRN's Kuala Lumpur leaders. A quiet reflective fella with fire in his eyes; reminded me of my slave driver SO during training.

Moktar/Kamal's eyes wrinkled in laughter.

The four of us had a teh tarik conversation that lasted for about two hours. They made it seem like it was merely chitchat, but I could see they were probing and feeling me out. As planned, I dropped the fact that I took part in a supply run in Central Firdaus, was separated from the others when I sustained injuries, and snuck into a medical center to give myself first aid, escaping a few days later. That due to my having missed my job for four days, my Firdaus employment agency dropped me like a hot potato. I spoke passionately of hatred towards Governor Ting and the Firdaus establishment, how downtrodden folks at Tanah were.

He gave a long sigh.

I think they bought it. Marcus mentioned at the end that he'd be in touch. Let's see what happens...

Moktar/Kamal lifted his head, looking directly into an unseen camera, his brown eyes wrinkled with laughter.

Hey, David, you watching this?

He frowned and then leaned closer.

Make sure you delete this from the record, man.

His face lit up instantaneously.

I got to tell you, Dave, being in a young body is fabulous! I'd forgotten how tired I was all the time. This Kamal guy is fit and ripped, bro! I run for miles every morning and don't even get winded! Dahsyat, man!

He shook his head.

And he's quite the horndog. Jogged by a hot girl that day and got a boner the size of the Titanic. I swear I'm a hormonal teenager!

After a couple of minutes he sobered up, wiping dampness from his eyes. When his face was revealed to the camera, it was once again serious and collected.

Moktar Ghazali signing off.

The holographic image disappeared.

HOLOGRAPHIC TRANSMISSION
To: Special Branch HQ, Firdaus Central
From: Insp. Moktar Ghazali, #1834858
Date: 29 January 2089, 17:24hrs

Moktar/Kamal's attention was on something to the side of the unseen camera, before he stood back, rolling his head on his shoulders as he stood facing them.

The evening after my transmission last week, I was collected by Joe and brought to the KRN headquarters in blindfold. It was more than an hour's journey, but with numerous twists and turns on the way. I believe a significant number of these turns were bogus attempts to disorient me. I am unable to pinpoint the actual location.

He grimaced, obviously disappointed with himself.

I have been brought there three times this week, including the first trip. All under blindfold. Sometimes it was with Joe as my guide, sometimes Prabhat. Each time, Marcus was there to greet me, and he would be surrounded by a dozen or so other people. I would say I have met approximately 70 KRN members so far. The first two occasions I entered the headquarters, I merely sat in their group meeting, where they discussed consolidation and distribution of the food resources. All very innocuous. No talk of active terrorism whatsoever.

The third evening, there was the largest crowd thus far—about 40 that time—and they were having a social gathering. Mostly it was young people, aged between their twenties to forties. Marcus was there, and a few other elders, but I was not introduced to them. The congregation was singing, dancing and chanting, creating weird music using rudimentary instruments. I've never heard those kinds of rich melodies before...

His eyes glazed over as he stared off-camera. Then he seemed to refocus and resumed his attention to the transmission.

I think it's opportune for me to inform the administration of the sad state of the Tanah dwellers' food supply.

He spoke, his tone hard and emotionless, as if delivering a standard line in the Force's Code of Allegiance. But his eyes glittered with emotion.

I saw women and children, emaciated from hunger and diseased from lack of medical attention. And the people living in my neighborhood, unrelated to KRN activities, are starving too. I gave away half of my weekly rations to a family next door. For some reason, their handicapped son, who's living with them, is not allocated any rations. Not even disability benefits. That's just not right…

He shook his head. Then Moktar/Kamal blinked, lifting his chin to the screen, excitement lighting up his eyes.

If a message could be left for me, here at this transmission center, about how to drop off extra supplies, I can arrange for them to flow back into the community.

He stopped, biting his lip, then wiped his face with his hands aggressively as he cleared his throat.

I know I may be overstepping my bounds. But I just wanted to put my recommendation on record.

Then Moktar/Kamal hardened his features and began to recite monotonously, his deep youthful voice lacking in inflection.

The KRN headquarters is underground, I believe somewhere within the old connecting tunnel roadways or water drainage tunnels. The place where they held the social is a large space, about four stories high. And the participants of the dance and song were gathered in the bottom central area, spectators standing along guarded rails all the way up. Here...

He turned his palm forward and put it up towards the camera, obscuring himself in the background. Slowly, he scrolled through four pictures.

The first was of a crowd of about 20 young people, men and women, dressed in street clothes, dancing about, obviously having a good time. Moktar/Kamal was clearly standing a few stories above them, as the shot was an aerial view.

The second picture was across the distance to a railing where four men and two women stood, smiling and clapping as they watched the performance below, the heads of the performers situated at the bottom of the shot.

The third picture was a close-up of a cluster of older men standing slightly apart from the crowd facing the performers. Marcus Nara stood prominently in the center, a good half-foot taller than the tallest of the men surrounding him. The cluster seemed to be in deep discussion, while their eyes remained on the entertainment.

The final picture was of an empty tunnel with poor lighting. One could barely make out on the left a shelving unit bearing cardboard boxes of unknown content, and below, the tarmac bearing the faint remnants of yellow epoxy-painted road markings.

The last one was of the route they took me out from. I took this while I was blindfolded, but they restrained my wrists after, so I didn't manage to get any other usable photographs.

Moktar/Kamal released a long sigh as he blinked, obviously trying to recall if there was anything else to report. He rubbed his face, before turning back to the camera.

I'm scheduled to go there again in a couple of days, and will update in the next transmission.

He hesitated, his brown eyes flickering to the camera, then his gaze brightened.

I await arrangements for the sending of supplies here. Until then, this is Moktar Ghazali, signing off.

The hologram blinked off.

ACP Gomez shifted in his seat to the side of the holographic transmitter.

"Obviously, sir, we did not take any steps to provide the assistance Moktar requested."

CP Badrul lifted his chin in understanding. Although Firdaus administration made a brouhaha about community support, it was actually unheard of for Firdaus to lend any meaningful assistance to the Tanah folk. Each level had its own depository of supplies, and their supply hoard was necessary for the Firdaus residents. If the Tanah folk wanted more, they should first be prepared to lay down their arms, rat out the KRN for the nuisance that it was, and then maybe, just maybe, the Firdaus administration would see to a more even distribution of food supplies.

"Unfortunately, this was the response we received the following week."

ACP Gomez pressed a button to transmit the next holographic image.

HOLOGRAPHIC TRANSMISSION

To: Special Branch HQ, Firdaus Central

From: Insp. Moktar Ghazali, #1834858

Date: 5 February 2089, 09:05hrs

Front and center of the screen, the 3D image of Moktar/Kamal was of an impassive face, the countenance held still as he positioned himself upright to face the transmitter.

Moktar Ghazali on Day 21 of my undercover mission.

His voice was monotonous and hard.

No news of supplies, I see, nor any response to my request. I get the message. Nak seribu daya.

He blinked rapidly. For a moment the fleeting vision of the muscles in his youthful features clenching was detected. Moktar/Kamal rocked back on his heels, holding his shoulders erect.

I have nothing interesting to report. Signing off.

The hologram blanked abruptly, indicative of Moktar's growing insolence.

HOLOGRAPHIC TRANSMISSION
To: Special Branch HQ, Firdaus Central
From: Insp. Moktar Ghazali, #1834858
Date: 20 March 2089, 11:32hrs

Moktar/Kamal was dressed in a simple long-sleeved T-shirt, his face covered with a smattering of facial hair, and his hair long enough to curl around his collar.

Moktar Ghazali, on Day 49 of my mission.

His eyes flickered to the side, softening as he looked at something or someone off-screen.

My apologies for being unable to transmit for the past few weeks. I was involved in several activities with the KRN, including providing medical assistance and distributing supplies to the people at the Kampung Baru area who were hit by the flash floods. I had a few KRN members shadowing me, and it would have been too suspicious for me to return to the transmission area during that time.

He turned his palm forward and displayed a picture of a family standing knee-deep in muddied water, the children sharing a packet of rice cradled in an older woman's hands. He shook his hand, and another image presented itself: this time a picture of reddish-brown rooftops peeking through a flood of red muddied water.

I have seen with my own eyes the kind of camaraderie that exists between the people here in Tanah. They are hardened and rebellious, yes, but also courageous in their resolve to make do with the precious resources allocated to them. There is a sincerity in their interactions that I've never seen before.

But the Tanah people are beaten down by the system. Perhaps that is why the KRN gains ground, despite the aggressive campaigns we carry out to dissuade the public from associating with them. If I may be so bold, I would recommend that the Firdaus administration find a way to work with the KRN rather than against it. That would be a sure way of regaining the Tanah people's trust. And we can ensure a just distribution of supplies for everyone. We are all Malaysians after all…

Moktar/Kamal looked up again towards the point off-screen, his mouth pursed. Then he sighed.

I would volunteer to coordinate such efforts.

His voice reached a plateau towards the end, as if he realized the plea would fall on deaf ears.

The hologram blinked off.

"Sudahlah tu! That's it!" CP Badrul sat forward in his chair, his rounded tummy grazing the edge of the conference table. "It is obvious this naïve boy has become sympathetic to their plight. Instead of doing his job of infiltrating the KRN ranks and reporting back to us, he's now on a crusade to help the Tanah people!"

CP Badrul realized his voice was rising, and he sat back, taking a deep breath. "Harapkan pagar, pagar makan padi! It's obvious what needs to be done. We terminate this mission, and later, we'll plant someone else to plant the virus into the KRN network. Someone less susceptible to emotions. You!" He pointed a pudgy index finger towards the doctor. "Disconnect Inspector Moktar from the neurotransmitter immediately! Let his mind shrivel, the traitor!"

Dr. Varughese stepped forward, absent-mindedly rubbing a hand over his bald head, turning left and right towards ACP Gomez and SAC Ho.

"What?" CP Badrul barked out, his temperature rising at the insolence of his inferiors. "Someone tell me what the fuck is going on!" He no longer made any attempt to control the volume of his voice. His face was now flushed in anger, sweat glittering in his salt-and-pepper hair.

ACP Gomez stepped forward instead. “Sir, a KRN entry happened last night, or should I say early morning, and as at 03:45 hours, Moktar’s body was removed from the Cyberbotics Center.”

CP Badrul’s fist banged against the conference table, making the holographic transmitter rattle in its spot.

“Utter incompetence!” CP Badrul rose awkwardly from his seat, and started making his way to the door.

“Wait, sir!” SAC Ho shouted out, causing CP Badrul to pause in his maneuver around the edge of the conference table. “We have one last transmission to show you. We received it mid-morning today.”

CP Badrul waved his hand dismissively, his angered mind now merely interested in finding some peace from this catastrophe.

HOLOGRAPHIC TRANSMISSION

To: Special Branch HQ, Firdaus Central

From: Insp. Moktar Ghazali, #1834858

Date: 15 April 2089, 11:32hrs

I saw the historical pictures, you bastards!

The voice of Moktar/Kamal spoke without preamble, his holographic image facing straight ahead towards them.

Marcus showed me all the newspaper cuttings from 2034, of how Governor Ting was in fact in the same political party as Marcus before the Bersatu Coalition won their majority seats. The Bersatu manifesto set out a plan for a new, safer dwelling for everyone in Firdaus, not a select rich few! The promises they made to win the elections! Laknat!

Things we were never taught in school. Fiction, music and arts. Not the bland scratchings you guys called art, but real emotional stuff. But you can't have that, can you? No! The arts encouraged people to think for themselves. The arts made people query their surroundings, hope for a better future, rather than lie down and take the scraps that you throw at them. And to think that it is the Firdaus computer system that is supposed to ensure a fair distribution of resources!

Moktar/Kamal's eyes glistened with determination, his shoulders squared as though challenging all the police officers in the transmission room to enter his transmitter station for a hand-to-hand fight.

Well, I'm going to do everything in my power to ensure this abuse of power desists immediately!

His declaration carried a foreboding ring as the holographic transmission ended.

Mere seconds after the final transmission ended, a loud blaring alarm shattered the gaping silence of the conference room. Everyone looked up and around, distressed at the unfamiliar sound. A flat computerized voice which everyone immediately identified as the Firdaus AI control center then made a loud announcement:

"Complete system failure. Complete system failure."

Just as swiftly, the lights in the conference room blinked off, and in their place, the dull glow of one emergency lamp emitted over the large space.

"Bodoh!" CP Badrul shouted out, as the other police officers started scrambling towards the exit to rescue themselves. "You put the cyber weapon into the hands of KRN, you imbecile! He's gone and inserted the virus into Firdaus's system, not theirs!"

Unusual Suspects

×

TARIQ KAMAL

The Greater Klang Valley Metropolitan Area.

But of course no one calls it that. After the sinking of Klang and Kuala Selangor, the evacuations, the re-consolidation, the foreign money pouring in, the petitions for corporate sovereignty, the reconstruction, the demographic upheaval, bubble and crash, only Kolumpo remains. Four thousand plus square kilometers of urban sprawl, 40 million plus souls, one-third of that existing in the margins, invisible.

Almost every kind of use for the land found its way into the heart of Kolumpo's muddy bowl, the result of the preceding chaos. It's a place to live, from the bottom of the slums of Kolumpo's Arkologi Rakyat, the closeted and insular Kampungs and Tamans, enclaves on guard from the outside world, to the glittery heights of the arcologies of Fairmontshire and Effingham Place, tourist playgrounds for the rich, famous and worthy. It's millions of acres of farmland, from on-the-grid Monsanto and AgroTek vertical farms, powered by distant nuclear reactors, to quietly hidden, off-the-grid hydroponics growing patent-violating and illegal goods, run on surreptitious tidal generators buried in the muddy heart of the city. It's coldly efficient labs and offices and run-down backyard shops run beneath the notice of local law or any law. All underneath a sky where neither stars nor orbital ring can be seen, drowned by the light from neon, OLED and metamaterial unifog—all ads, all frantically selling something: the promise of beautiful and perfect bodies to own or to be; of holidays to Antarctica and outer space; of the latest toy or app; of that old Malaysian staple, food.

All of this flowed past Garrett Bryn's awareness, as his eyes stared out of the window of the transport-drone. He had seen it before. To him, Kolumpo resembled Shenzhen resembled Seattle resembled Mumbai—grinding poverty pushing against technology and civilization. Only the details changed—history, the players, what was permitted and verboten, and new tech, like this t-drone.

The drone itself was one of the newer vac-dirigibles, quieter and more reliable than the older jet-powered hovercraft models. The seats were plush, and the guiding personality piloting the drone bland but pleasant. And since it was coming out of Dalvik-Tellus SA's expense account, it was completely free of charge.

Garrett sighed. DT had squared his debts, and, true to their word, had fixed him. Never mind the contractual agreements, at least the chronic pain from his old neural injury was gone—the one the doctors said couldn't be fixed, all those years ago. The one that had destroyed a promising career.

Not anymore. He could carry subsidiary personalities again, and the timeless ecstasy that came from every dive into Deep Data was his again.

He wasn't little people anymore, and man, did it feel good to be back on top.

"Situation report," said Garrett curtly, as he walked into DT's Business Continuity node, a hive of hastily patched together workstations and frenetic activity. He had wisely ditched his trenchcoat and suit for something a little cooler, more business casual, but he had kept his shades, which served as intimidation fodder, data source and augmented vision.

A middle-aged woman—the shades identified her as Lakshmi Gunasegaran, local Business Continuity Coordinator and Acting Operations Head—looked up from a discussion with several of her colleagues at Garrett for a few seconds, no doubt using that time to query the administrative artilect on who the hell was this Mat Salleh walking into *her* operations room.

She nodded. The local operations artilect—"case-boss"—had briefed her, quickly and silently. She made a call that Garrett knew she would—best to ditch formal greetings; no time.

"We're back up to 95% capacity," she began. "With maybe about three hours' worth of lost transactions in the City Center node."

"That's all?"

Lakshmi shook her head, frustrated. She was dressed in an all-white jumpsuit—DT's standard uniform—and it was clear that she had not slept in the past 24 hours.

"Yes," she said, sarcastically. "*Only* three hours' worth of lost transactions, at 15 billion credits an hour. *Only* half a dozen DT equity holders in hospital, their brains scrambled, so the highest level of purchasing authority we have in this country is me, and they're still revoking and reissuing the keys to upgrade me to country manager when what we need to resolve this quickly is a Regional Vice President. *Only* the servers in Central are fried—we've only got the backups loaded and started after several hours of borrowing and patching equipment.

"At least data storage is intact, thank God, and it *only* got wiped clean. At least we could get a copy of the case-boss running locally on our qubit array, so it doesn't have to deal with *only* network latency. We're *only* failing almost all of our metrics. Hooray!"

Garrett ignored her seething anger, and pressed on. "No logs?"

"Nothing. Don't you listen? Storage got *wiped*, remember?"

Garrett cursed. "What about our security situation? Is it likely we'll be hit by another attack?"

"Not likely," said Lakshmi, a little more composed and abashed after her outburst. "Intrusion countermeasures are up, and you're expected to follow the security policies until the disaster is declared over. Case-boss is enforcing it for us right now, and if it notices any hanky-panky from any of us it's authorized to knock us out first, ask questions later."

"Got it. Any evidence? I'd like to review the materials, since I couldn't see a lot of them on the way here."

"Almost nothing. It happened at night, on a public holiday. No one in the office. Only person who could have seen anything was downstairs, at the mall. Maintenance and facilities for the shopping kiosks, graveyard shift."

"The witness statement, then?" said Garrett. "I skimmed the video, but it was a low-bandwidth preview."

"Well, today's your lucky day, then," said Lakshmi. "We've got the high-def stuff hosted on the local intranet. Go ahead and jack in."

"Okay, we're recording your statement now."

The video wasn't made in some government lock-up. For one, the facilities looked clean and well-maintained, and for another, the metadata streaming in was high-quality, corporate-grade. The interviewers were off-camera, but Garrett caught a glimpse of their uniforms. Not local cops—likely DT polis bantuan. The anachronistically named *Royal* Malaysian Police? Only there as observers, since it was a matter of corporate sovereignty.

"Okay. Um, I was running through a checklist, and making sure that the volatiles that the kiosks needed were stocked up..."

The subject of the video was a woman in her mid-twenties. A local, judging by her dark brown skin color and accent. Plain, somewhat dumpy, which was why she was on the graveyard shift, away from the customers. Dressed in grey holding facility overalls. Wearing an underscarf, which Garrett figured was part of DT's concession to political correctness.

Garrett rolled his eyes. This crap was frankly beneath him. He quickly redirected the video to the background of his consciousness, and delegated the task of transcribing to Colonel Mustard, the subsidiary personality that served as his amanuensis. As an afterthought, he shunted the sensor data measuring the subject's physical responses to the other sub-personality regular in his head, Parry, who lived for obsessively digging through reams of data to look for anything suspicious.

Garrett yawned as he pulled the interface helmet from his face and stood up. The office cubicles around him were empty, but he spotted Lakshmi's office, which was lit up and occupied.

Walking in, he caught Lakshmi concluding a phone call.

"...all right. Tell our son that Mama's still not gonna be done until later today. Love you too, babe. B'bye."

Garrett smirked. "Trouble at home?"

Lakshmi gave Garrett a long, even stare. "Nothing unusual in our line of work," she said, finally. "You weren't out for long. Anything insightful in that witness report?"

Garrett shrugged. "Working on it right now; figured I didn't need anything more than wireless connectivity for the time being. Is that all, though? What about the equity holders? Are they awake already?"

Lakshmi grunted. “Funny you should mention that,” she said. “The doctors say they’re still out—whatever it was, it hit them pretty hard. Catatonia, aphasia, seizures, the lot. They’re saying that we might need to restore them from their daily backups.”

Garrett pursed his lips, irritated. “If we have to resort to flashing from nightlies, they won’t remember anything from the day before the attacks. We’ll get nothing.”

“Yep. You want the medical reports; see if they make sense to you?”

“Yeah, sure,” said Garrett. “Send them to my inbox. I’ll check in and work from the hotel.”

Garrett stared moodily at the constellation of data painstakingly assembled in front of him.

After piping in both the mnemonic transcript that Colonel Mustard had gathered, and the annotations that Parry had obsessively overlaid on it, Garrett wasn’t anywhere near figuring out what had happened, much less figuring out what to do.

Floating in the void he had cleared out in his superconsciousness, Garrett looked at the first piece of information he had: an analysis of the malformed data cascade that caused the incident. The first linkage for this data came early in the investigation, while he was reading the briefing, on a plane from Bao’an to KLIA Island.

It resembled a neurasthenic cascade failure of MIT's early upload experiments, during the first few tentative years of what could have been the transhumanist gold rush.

That would have been an odd coincidence to a historical footnote, were it not for the medical reports of the DT equity holders that Lakshmi piped in several hours later. It took a while to decipher—Garrett had ended up spending a good half-day integrating a subsidiary personality that had the required knowledge into his mind—but then he realized he was looking at something impossible: NCF happening inside a human brain.

He pulled himself out of the data trance, and the void collapsed around him, revealing his hotel room. It had this retro, grody look, with period-era signs that were apparently real vintage (nothing says vintage, ironic or not, like "WHITES ONLY"), but at least it had the data services he needed.

"Hey, phone," he said to thin air. "Call the case-boss."

Silence for a few minutes as his communicator negotiated the connections and authentication needed. Then the icon of the DT artilect in charge of the case materialized in front of him.

"GREETINGS, MR. BRYN," said the artilect, in a neutral, beige-sounding voice. "WHAT CAN I DO TO ASSIST YOU?"

"Yeah, I'm looking for someone attached to this case who's an expert on upload tech and neuromedicine," said Garrett.

"WOULD THE CURRENT DT R&D HEAD BE USEFUL FOR YOUR PURPOSES?"

Garrett nodded, and waited as the DT artilect made the necessary connections. His gaze caught the digital clock displaying the time, and he noticed that the clock was showing 5:00am only before Dr. Elker Grunewald, head of DT R&D, materialized. A woman in her early fifties, she had elected to crop her hair short, and her expression was stern, businesslike.

"Ah, Dr. Grunewald, I apologize for calling you so late—"

"No matter," said the doctor, curtly. "We've had late shifts here in Zurich, and I was just about to sign out before your case-boss messaged me. What's another call?"

"Well, Doctor," said Garrett, "I'm forwarding you some data on our ongoing investigation…"

Garrett waited while Dr. Grunewald perused the data. "I'm sorry, but I don't understand why you need my expertise here. This is a classic NCF."

"Except that one occurred in an urban populated area," said Garrett. "And the other isn't an engram representation of machine failure. It's from a human brain."

Dr. Grunewald's eyebrows raised in surprise. "You must be joking! NCF on organic brains?"

Garrett felt Parry, who had this habit of eavesdropping on the conversations Garrett had with people when he wasn't busy, shift in his head.

She's being too blasé about NCF, he heard Parry say, unbidden. *NCFs don't happen on anything except dedicated data nodes, away from residential populations. Don't like people hiding stuff from us. Call her out on it.*

"I'm sorry, Doctor Grunewald," said Garrett. "But I noticed your lack of surprise."

"Eh?"

"Uploads are held in data nodes away from people, Doctor. Power and cooling requirements, and the potential danger."

Dr. Grunewald looked uncomfortable at Garrett's questioning. "…Yes. It is unusual…"

"Current literature is clear, doctor: uploads take a lot of juice, and tend to fail explosively. Thus, they are kept away from where people live and work. Unless you know something we don't, which I think you do," said Garrett. "May I remind you that I am currently investigating a case against the corporate personhood of your employer, ma'am, and that you're *required* to not withhold any information from me?"

"Absolutely," said Dr. Grunewald, rattled, her steely exterior beginning to crack, finally showing her exhaustion. "Then please understand that this piece of information is strictly in confidence. You know the history of human uploads, of course, and why research in that area petered out."

Garrett nodded. It was common knowledge, history.

Sadly, the dream of mind uploads—of immortality and freedom from our flesh—fell short, as the kind of hardware that was needed to operate the human mind was prohibitively expensive—surprisingly so, since the human brain could do it with far less, and didn't require materials that needed their own power plants, cooling towers and hundreds of layers of ballistic foam.

One part of the problem was that the human mind—or at least the thing that other human minds recognized as a "human mind"—was basically the human brain. And the human brain was a picky, temperamental thing. It needed a body, and that body needed an environment, and that environment had to be real enough. It was an iron-clad chain of requirements that resisted every attempt at pruning. Attempts to do so always ended up like trying to defuse a bomb in an old skool Hollywood action video by cutting the red wire…while blind. Also, the bomb kept reconfiguring itself, often without you noticing.

And the price of cutting the wrong wire? Neural cascade failures. At best, you got minds that were stuck in catatonia, folded into themselves, irrevocably mad. At worst? You had the kind of nasty malware that caused the 'Net to shatter—that still remained, to this day, blights in what should have been a consensual hallucination open to all of humanity.

"As you know, the only people who have been uploaded and remain operating are the point-oh-one percenters," said Dr. Grunewald. "Even then, the yearly operations costs are staggering. All that energy wasted on cooling and more memory banks as the mind expands. They weren't even any smarter, so no value there. If you're a foundation stuck with running these minds, you had two options: disown them or run out of money. It was an intractable problem…"

"...until now."

"Not...quite," she said. "We wondered...you know, maybe we shouldn't try to do all the uploading all at once. Upload them a little, a bit at a time. Let the brain do some of the pruning work for us."

"Yes...?"

"The problem was, you know, you couldn't do that with just anyone. Normal adult brains aren't plastic enough. You know, like yours, it has some plasticity, but what we were looking to do, at least in the early stages, you couldn't have survived it."

"So how did you solve it?"

"Well...we needed to locate a subject, and you know how governments here are," said Dr. Grunewald. "The EU wouldn't allow this sort of research, the American States have a host of objections, religious as well as the usual ethical ones, and the Japanese...well, the Japanese were willing, but they wanted the technology to remain theirs. So we resorted to countries that DT had corporate sovereignty in. Which included Malaysia."

"I don't like how this is turning out, but go on."

"Well, the research operations runs highly autonomously over there for obvious reasons, but we just received the research notes from that branch on the eve of this attack. We were going to incorporate them into the case-boss's reports, but only after going through them. And that's why we were up late, verifying the findings."

"All right," said Garrett. "What have you found?"

"R&D had been running this operation for over two decades," said Dr. Grunewald. "And they had found a promising batch of subjects from a group of climate-change refugees. At an orphanage."

"Wait a minute. You said, earlier on, 'normal adult brains'. Are you saying that this research involved—"

"Yes. An elective nanotechnological neural prosthetics regimen, administered from infancy onwards."

"You were operating on the brains of children."

"Not exactly *us*, you understand...but yes."

Garrett read the reports, and despite everything, winced. The results of the "nanotechnological neural prosthetics regimen", as Dr. Grunewald bloodlessly named it, tended to be grisly, if not downright horrific. In some, the phage failed to integrate, causing devastating immunological responses. In others, it integrated too well, creeping up the spinal cord and into the brain, causing early dementia and eventually death. Every developmental milestone was potentially a trap, every physiological change an invitation to disaster.

Out of two dozen children, half died during childhood. Another six passed away during puberty. Three survived into neural maturity, but only one was considered a suitable candidate.

Garrett looked at the file image of the candidate, prior to the operation: a dark-skinned young man, just over the age of 24. His final medical report showed it all: rather than a tangled thicket of synapses and connections that came naturally through organic processes, the brain had done most of the work of simplification over the years, until only a few dozen connections were left, and it had organized itself beautifully. A modular brain, with a fully functioning mind.

He was perfect—estimates were that the resulting upload would be hundreds of times smaller and run on less resources than whatever they had on file.

"So what happened to the upload itself?"

"That's the thing," said Dr. Grunewald. "The final scan went without a hitch. The results were better than expected—the resulting upload was only several times larger than a typical subsidiary personality, very much in the middle ranges of the artilect scale, but theoretically much more capable. That's not very large, but it's too large to run off by itself. It needs qubit storage, it can't archive itself and run off without the help of confederates—"

"So it—*he* had help. Are all the members of the local R&D branch accounted for?"

"Yes," said Dr. Grunewald. "Either reassigned, retired under invasive surveillance, or liquidated."

Silence from Garrett's side. "The other subjects? The ones who also made it to adulthood?"

"There were two others," said Dr. Grunewald. "You have seen their records. Also liquidated."

Something bothered Garrett about that. Something—

He had a sudden feeling of dread; a realization that he had made a terrible mistake. He opened the archives, digging through the records, photos of the subjects, until—

"One of the subjects is still alive, Dr. Grunewald," he said, before terminating the connection and summoning the DT artilect.

"Call operations and the holding center, case-boss," he said. "Our suspect's the maintenance girl."

"What do you mean, she's been released?"

Garrett glared at Lakshmi, who returned Garrett's stare with a measured, scornful indifference. Next to her, the security forces liaison, a police officer in his late twenties, fidgeted uneasily.

"Released per our sovereignty agreement with local authority," she said, narrowing her eyes. "Her documentation all checks out, anyway, and she has no outstanding warrants—"

"Of course she doesn't," snapped Garrett. "Her documentation, her clean record...*fake*! Her rap sheet—her real one—was a mile long! Fraud, forgery, hacking, identity theft: it was just as well she was earmarked as one of our assets, or she'd be in Sungai Buloh, rotting in some jail cell. And *no one* recognized her?"

Silence from Lakshmi, as she pursed her lips and looked at her pad.

"We have bigger problems, Garrett. If you haven't noticed, we are barely able to *run our business*," she said, and Garrett noticed the bulging vein on her forehead, the gritted teeth, her fingers digging into the pad. "We're still struggling to hit break-even without the additional cost of feeding and holding some fucking nobody. So we let her go. And then you barged in, saying we shouldn't. Okay, great. She just left. 15 minutes ago."

"Wait, 15 minutes? That means—"

"ON IT," chirruped the DT artilect into a headpiece in Garrett's ear. "QUERYING LOCAL AUTHORITIES... SURVEILLANCE LOCATES HER 200 METERS AWAY FROM THE SENTUL ENTRANCE OF THE ARKOLOGI RAKYAT."

Looking at the liaison, Garrett asked, "She's our top suspect. Do you have anyone out there?"

The liaison nodded. "That area's crowded, though. Finding her will be impossible without—"

"I have it," snapped Lakshmi, coming off her communicator. "You've got three squadrons of cam-drones, and we've interfaced with local police control."

"Good," said Garrett. "We need her alive, you understand? She's the one who'll lead us to our asset."

Stepping out of the t-drone, Garrett was hit, for the first time, by the full force of Kolumpo's heat and humidity.

Lakshmi observed him with sardonic amusement. "First time out in Kolumpo's weather?"

Garrett grunted, ignoring her jibe. "What's the current status of our target?"

"She got into the complex before we could block her way," she said, as the both of them walked to a nearby police hut, manned by a police officer. "Just a few minutes ago."

Garrett felt a pang of despair, and groaned. "In the arcology already? Do you have any presence in there at all?"

"Not a lot," said the police officer—Royal Police, this time—shaking his head. "We have outposts, but they're too few and far between. Luckily she entered in an area that we have some control over, but it's nominal. Near the edges. She'll be out of range if we don't move now."

"Good enough. Get the cam-drones in and scout ahead. Case-boss?"

"YES, MR. BRYN."

"Link with the cops. Then take point and lead us where to go."

X

Imagine if someone had taken the old Kowloon Walled City, made it cover the entirety of Sentul, parts of Bukit Tunku and Bukit Ceylon, all of Kampung Datuk Keramat and chunks of Kampung Baru, with tendrils towards the KL City Center and Bukit Bintang.

Imagine all of that, and you've imagined Kolumpo's Arkologi Rakyat: an ironic, belated name, given late in its life, after it had swallowed chunks of Jalan Kuching and Tun Razak.

In its heart, it is rumored, lies the Titiwangsa Lake; there are no records of what the lake looks like now, only grainy videos of doubtful veracity made by urban explorers. The buildings that now cover it have in part a life of their own, thanks to the imperfect yet persistent nanotechnology that brought them into existence: manic construction turning into a cancerous nightmare, thankfully stopped in other places, but too late for the complex of buildings that eventually formed Kolumpo's AR. Electric pylons surround the land now, keeping the infestation of buildings at bay, and the arcology remains quiet, perhaps realizing that it will only be tolerated so long as it does not escape the boundaries it has claimed.

Having given up on administering the buildings, city authorities try in vain to keep in check the people who have made the AR their home. But hampered by their powerlessness in the face of corporate sovereignty, which sees the AR as an ever-replenishing pool of human resources and cheap labor, the iron laws of demographics, and the belated consequences of neglect, they can do little. The arcology is a land which creates its own laws and is perversely self-sufficient—it nourishes and powers itself from flood waters, it steals bandwidth from the infosphere, and every inch of the way, resists surveillance and pacification.

And into one of its warrens, a squad of heavily armed soldiers, led by a swarm of camera drones, makes their painstaking way.

"CAMERA DRONE SIGHTS TARGET 150 METERS AWAY, MR. BRYN."

Garrett nodded, throat suddenly dry, and gestured to the squad of police he led. Garrett's sunglasses, which provided him with infrared vision, also told him that both he and the squad he was with had been in the arcology for almost an hour, although it had felt, strangely, longer.

The atmosphere within the arcology was cooler than the outside world. Garrett and the police had initially passed through the eerily silent living areas of the arcology—the inhabitants had wisely hidden themselves rather than confront the armed team. Then, a section with giant, humming machinery.

Now they were deep within the silent guts of the arcology, buried in civilization yet isolated.

Garrett swallowed uneasily, needled by a feeling he could not put into words. The buzz of the infosphere, a constant companion to him these few weeks, was reduced to the merest whispers now, maintained by a thin lifeline, existing by the sheer force of will of the artilect.

"SHE'S UP AHEAD, MR. BRYN, AT THE EDGE OF THE CLIFF."

"Cliff?" asked Garrett under his breath.

"A STORM CANAL, SIR," said the artilect. "500-METER DROP. I'VE INSTRUCTED THE SQUAD TO CUT OFF OTHER AVENUES OF ESCAPE."

Garrett nodded, and signaled to secure the area and make sure that their quarry didn't escape. Ahead, he spotted the small, marble-sized camera drones, and in the darkness, the heat-image of his target—a short, pudgy girl wearing a hijab and her work uniform, complete with apron. She stood, leaning at the rail near the lip of the canal, and alternately peering into the darkness ahead of her and at the steep drop behind her.

Belatedly, Garrett noticed that his target was holding a handset up to her ear, talking to someone. Idly, he wondered why. There was no other bandwidth available this deep into the arcology. The only connectivity was what DT, with the artilect's silent coordination, brought in here. They had passed the last inhabited area forty minutes ago.

The needling unease rose to a pitch, became anxiety. It looked as if she was—

"AS IF SHE IS ON THE PHONE WITH SOMEONE, MR. BRYN? BUT WHO? A 'CONFEDERATE', AS THE GOOD DOCTOR SAID?"

Garrett started. It was the DT artilect, the case-boss, its voice suddenly gaining human qualities he had never noticed before.

"Wait a minute—"

"ASTUTE AS EVER, MR. BRYN. BUT SADLY…"

Garrett remembered Lakshmi's words: about how everything but the qubit storage was wiped clean, including their records; how distracted operations were; that details were missed out, because DT was hemorrhaging money by the second; about how the upload was like an artilect but *more capable*; about how the case-boss, an artilect, held the keys to security, including the ability to knock out anyone "at the first sign of hanky-panky", because everyone else was trying to get higher-value work done, like struggling to get DT to just break even—

But…too late, he realized, as his awareness was filled with a burst of nonsense, as Colonel Mustard was stabbed in the library with a candlestick, and Parry went to the horse races to get shot by the mafia—

It was too late, he thought, as he dreamily saw the police officers, their brains patched in as well, convulse and fall—

"…LATE TO THE PARTY."

White noise.

Tasha put down the handset and peered into the darkness.

The camera drones had seized up and fallen, their delicate electronics mangled. She could also hear the muffled grunts and gasps of the squad that was pursuing her, and watched as some weasel-faced bastard, dressed in a ludicrous Hawaiian shirt and fucking sunglasses (sunglasses in the middle of a place that never saw sunlight, really?), fall down along with them.

She lifted up the handset and asked the person on the other end of the line, "It's done?"

"Dah," said the voice on the handset, which sounded more like Irfan now. "They're out, and I finally got the key to all their brains. Sorry I had to involve you in this, Akak."

"Takper," said Tasha, as she cradled the headset again. "So…what now?"

"Well, I've cleared a route for you to the gang," he said. "The taikors all won't remember Friday. These fellers are going to wake up remembering something suitably dramatic that'll get them to stop kacau-ing you—"

"How lah?"

"Something drama," said Irfan, amused. "You cabut lari, they chase, you slip…masuk gaung. Too dark to see. Tragis. Mayat takder. And then, kasi lead, a nice wild goose chase across the world. Thanks to your lanun work with the security keys, I ikut sama, one step ahead, until…apa-apa je lah. See how. Amacam?"

"Dangerous lah," said Tasha, concerned.

"Akak," said Irfan, teasingly. "Dah terlambat nak risau the likes of me. I'm already dead, remember? Diorang nak buat apa lagi?"

"Don't say that; please don't say that," Tasha said, nodding, her eyes wet. "I'll miss you, adik. You give them hell for as long as you can, okay?"

Irfan laughed. "You bet I will, Akak."

The White Mask

×

ZEDECK SIEW

The White Mask is dead. Social media has the story before the cops find his body.

Now the news sites are all posting the same thing, the same photo, the same angle, taken from across the lanes—

Of the White Mask sitting slumped against the highway wall, wearing a black hoodie; black skinny jeans with both legs splayed; black sneakers. And at his feet: three loose curbstones, kicked out of their spaces.

He wears a white mask over his face, and a crushed and crinkled larynx.

Behind him, on the highway wall:

Dr. M, the Tun Doctor, standing as a stenciled mural. This is the Tun Doctor in the later years: in a Nehru collar; hands clasped together and hair combed back; cheeks and jowls sagging; small eyes framed by spectacles. Smiling with a hint of teeth showing.

I walk across as my online self. There are voices like a semicircle choir sighing around the body. "Was it a robbery?" somebody says, and somebody else says: "Was it an accident?"

A third somebody says: "Why are people posting this picture, dead people are not things I want to see at breakfast or anytime ever, stop posting this picture please or you will. Get. Blocked!"

There is a satchel of art supplies open on the ground; there are spray-paint cans rolled into corners.

I kneel to look at a can. At this zoom level the resolution is poor—but I already know what its label says:

Smart acrylic lacquer. Latest version, industry-standard, black in color.

And there is a live-stream now. We watch the cops watching the surveillance feed—

Of the White Mask, standing between pools of street-lamp light, facing the highway wall. He shakes his spray can. We can imagine what that sounds like: clickity clack-clack-clack.

The White Mask rolls his white undercoat onto the wall. It is an out-of-the-way wall, mostly empty—so this is a personal project, a minor independent commission maybe, an experiment.

The only thing already there is a graffiti tag, half-buried beneath the White Mask's new canvas. "Terror Thursday," the tag says, broody, squirming, trying to wriggle itself back to the surface—but it's a years-old thing, done in outdated hardware, its pigments unable to compete with the latest paints.

Piece by piece, the White Mask tapes up his stencil scaffold. His spray can sneezes, hisses—

The footage fast-forwards. His arms are a blur. They slow down again only as he steps back. We admire the wall with him: there's that mural of the Tun Doctor there now, just as we see it the next morning, in photos with the White Mask's body lying there.

But for now the White Mask is still working. His spray can cackles: clickity-clack-clack-clack. He places a stencil atop the Tun Doctor's hair.

The cut-out outline of a fluffy cloud.

The White Mask works at it methodically, layer by layer, coat by coat, each a different color—

So the Tun Doctor wears a rainbow clown wig now.

"So who is this White Mask guy?" somebody says.

"Though he got what he deserved," somebody else says. "I feel sorry for his family, but really, how can anybody disrespect the Tun Doctor, who brought us development and prosperity, the greatest leader of our country?"

A third somebody says: "The White Mask is not a he, the White Mask is a she."

And then we notice that the Tun Doctor is angry. Small and squinty before, now the Tun Doctor's eyes blink quickly; the lines about the Tun Doctor's teeth turn into a snarl.

We notice—but the White Mask does not. He crouches, unfolding his last stencil. It is a piece of cardboard with a circle cut in the center:

A round nose.

He shakes a can of red paint: clickity-clack-clack—

Then he freezes.

The Tun Doctor's hands and arms are reaching out and off the highway wall's surface: two flat sheets of black matter, viscous, elbow-less, snaking out and grasping in boneless, alien ways.

His hood falls from his head. He struggles a little, his white mask shaking: no-no-no. He is being strangled. The Tun Doctor has him by his neck

The spray can drops, toppling other spray cans like a strike to bowling pins.

The White Mask is held back to the wall, unable to break away. He kicks and kicks and kicks. He kicks the loose curbstones out of their spaces.

After a while he stops kicking.

The Tun Doctor stands up, wiping away the rainbow clown hair with whip-like fingers. Then the Tun Doctor settles: hands clasped together, small eyes squinting. Saintly smiling, with a hint of teeth showing.

Smart paint technology. Motorized nano-particulates, germs of pigment—umber or arsenic or ultramarine—movement-capable, programmable, bearing networked memory full of commands and subroutines.

I am something of an expert; I did engineering in Korea, at a university where they developed the technology.

"All fun and moving!" I say. "See?"

This was five-six years ago. I tilt a ceramic tile to show the Datuk what I mean.

On my tile there is a cartoon figure running in a hamster wheel, and the painted wheel is turning—it isn't just an animation on a screen; the paint itself is shifting, spinning around the ceramic surface.

The little painted, panting man keeps up by running.

I made my little ceramic tile for our Majestic Place presentation. My tile gets us the job—our client the Datuk laughs, in love with its motile, cutting-edge novelty.

Our client the Datuk comes from the petro-gas company that owns Majestic Place—

"It's a petro-gas company!" Adam says. "So we have to fuck with them."

What we do with Majestic Place—it is all Adam's idea. We turn it into a phantasmagoria. On its sides we lay pipeline calligraphy. We build onion domes with smokestack minarets; traffic jams piercing candy smog; trains, planes and rocket ships; swirling firework landscapes.

No natural tones. No green except for the coughing cartoon stiffs lining up for caffeine shots, on the walls of the building's ground floor coffee place.

I tell our client the Datuk—I reassure him, saying: "Look, Datuk, you want to tell people that your company has a vision. This neon city, this is your vision! This is your future: bright, full of color, full of energy!"

Majestic Place is the first moving smart paint mural in the country. For this fact alone our client the Datuk is very happy.

Adam and I win Multimedia Campaign of the Year. During industry awards night Adam goes onstage to accept our trophy. He wears his white mask and I am whooping.

"Whoo!" Adam says, his arms up, his palms open. "Whoo!"

Our friends fist-bump us. We are heroes, power couple of the evening: celebrity artist and code genius. We've hoodwinked a petro-gas company, more or less: clothed their corporate offices in toxic-nightmare landscapes, and afterwards they paid us money.

There are those who are not so congratulatory. Look:

Five-six guys in the corner, drinking soda, feigning the barest minimum applause to be polite.

These guys. They are the Terror Thursday crew. They are jealous.

Adam was the White Mask—is the White Mask.

When Adam starts wearing his mask, he is sixteen. He tags walls in Wangsa Maju, where he lives; eventually the mask becomes his identity, his thing.

It helps him. He does not have an easy beginning.

In this time of our lives we have not yet met. Adam runs with Terror Thursday—right now they are just a bunch of boys searching for themselves by the river's concrete flood banks, in spray cans, in squelchy long-poled roller brushes.

They draw jumping skateboarders and zombie hordes; polyhedral letters saying "VOX" and "LIFE" and "MERDEKA RAYA"; they draw green-irised girls in red-and-white headscarves, pleading for peace to return in the Middle East.

Terror Thursday is what they call themselves—

Thursday—meaning Thursday evening specifically, which in religion counts as the start of Friday, part of the holy day: a time of noble thoughts and purity, of artful God-blessed jihad.

Terror—not meaning horror, but the word used in its celebratory sense, somebody seeing a burning piece, or a cool perspective-trick painting, and saying: "Wah, so terror!"

The name is Ghaf's idea.

Ghaf is a good-looking guy. He is proud of his skill. He is not the best artist among them—that's Adam—but he does know where to get speciality paints for lower-than-market prices. So he takes command.

"The signs were there," Adam tells me later. "Could already see the way Ghaf would go."

At the start, Adam and Ghaf are a thing. That's how Adam gets in.

Of course it doesn't last, and Adam stays with the Terror Thursdays only for a few more years. Boys of that kind, at that age? They don't understand.

The mask is Adam's way of coping. It is a physical symbol that his personhood is changeable. He doesn't have to be whatever other people see. More and more he says this aloud.

For Ghaf and the rest—

To them he is still a girl: just out of her school baju, stuffed into a beanie and baggy tee. They grow uncomfortable.

"You shouldn't, you know," Ghaf says. "You are a girl. God made you a woman. You cannot go against God."

"You like to talk about changing the world," Adam tells him.

"For the better!" Ghaf says. "Not like this, for the worse."

Nowadays Ghaf is balding early. He wears a goatee and a skullcap under his hoodie. He talks to a news reporter.

"She does not represent us," he says. "Yes, the White Mask is actually a she. She was born a woman. We grew up together. Her real name is Dyana, she used to run with our crew."

The five-six guys of Terror Thursday stand together, looking grim.

"This was before she got her sex change," Ghaf says. "She left our crew to become a tomboy and a liberal.

"This, insulting the greatest leader of our country?" He points at the Tun Doctor standing in the highway wall. "This is going too far. It's treasonous. Sacrilegious! We street artists, we are patriots. People have to know she does not represent us."

The cowards, crusading against the dead. I am thinking how Adam made it so easy for them, getting himself killed like this—so stupid. He let them win.

One headline says: **Artists, NGOs lodge police report against Dr. M clown mural.**

Cops: White Mask death a programming error, another headline says.

There is a live-stream of the police press conference, with an officer holding up a notebook they found in Adam's bag, and he is flipping through its pages—

It is a book of sketches. In it is Dr. M, the Tun Doctor, page after page, in spectacles and Nehru collar, in various poses:

In a clown's get-up; in a cap with three stars arranged in a triangle; in a dress. With a beer bottle. Sitting on the toilet, eyes shut tightly, straining. His hands on two handles of a motorbike, planking on the bike seat, his legs stretched out straight behind him.

A third headline says: **Respect the Tun Doctor, Minister reminds youth.**

A month ago, Adam opens the notebook with his Tun Doctor sketches to show me.

"I'm thinking we can put these up as stencils," he says.

When I see what he's drawn I look him in the eye, and I ask: "Why?"

"For fun," Adam says. "You know Terror Thursday got that contract with the Ministry, that history campaign for Merdeka month? 'Malaysian Heroes' featuring the Tun Doctor. That's Ghaf, no imagination. I want to fuck with him."

"You'll piss off other people, not just Ghaf," I say. "They'll say you're insulting our greatest leader."

And Adam says: "So fuck them too."

"We won't even get paid for it. I don't think it's worth the trouble."

"And fuck you too!" Adam says.

Now, when I am not crying, I am thinking. If I'd been there I could have double-checked the paint's programming—

Smart paint stores commands and algorithms in its memory. The latest versions come with inbuilt anti-vandalism subroutines, so that paintings shield themselves from damage.

An authorized user inputs the desired level of security.

Whether the paint reacts to touch, reacts to the application of additional coats or colors, reacts to differing or knock-off brands. Whether it responds by dissolving foreign particulates—as the Tun Doctor did with Adam's clown wig.

Or by forcibly removing the source of attack—by physically debilitating attackers, for example.

Adam, he's not so good at code. He didn't program his paint properly—didn't properly add himself to the permissions list—so his own paint saw him as an attacker, and his own paint attacked him.

Me? Programming is my thing. If I'd been there—

The reason why industry-standard paint has anti-vandalism software:

Businesses think their marketing campaigns need protecting.

They need us. The Public Advertisements Act banned billboards in the late 2010s—but what we do, technically it isn't advertising. It is art. Corporate-sponsored art.

People like the Datuk and his petro-gas company—they pay us good money for our murals. More than anybody else, they don't want to wake up in the morning to see their branding defaced.

I remember Adam ranting about the money.

"The money is spoiling us," Adam says. "Just now I met Ruby, buying groceries, she asked why we've not visited her lately. Rich people already, is it, she said. She's right! In the past five-six years we've not done any work but corporate jobs—not one! When did we become corporate people?"

"Remember we've got a meeting with the Datuk tomorrow," I say.

We meet for the first time at a party at Ruby's place.

Adam is pretty: he has an angular face, curly hair; he wears a jean jacket, a smile that is sweet, half-cocky.

He wears a binder for his chest. He tells me about himself—about the Terror Thursdays and the work; about the White Mask; about going to court tomorrow, to show support for the trans women appeal case.

I tell him about my studies abroad in engineering. We talk about the future.

And five-six months later, even though he has me blindfolded I know he's brought me to the river—I can smell its stink.

"Surprise," he says.

Across the water, on the concrete flood bank, he's written his name and my name. Big block letters. Between those two words he's painted a heart. It is big, valved, bloody red.

I imagine it beating.

"Wipe out all of the White Mask's murals!" somebody says.

Somebody else replies: "I don't agree with his actions, but you know, as the French philosopher Voltaire says—"

The Datuk from the petro-gas company writes to tell me: "We have partnered with the White Mask crew for our Majestic Place premises for the past seven years. We feel now it is time to make a change.

"Please accept our sincerest thanks for what has been a warm, long and fruitful relationship. We wish you all the best!"

And in a separate message:

"I am so very sorry for your loss. You know, I liked you two very much, and I still do. But this recent thing, it's bothering my bosses a lot, they don't want the company seen associating with you. I hope you understand."

The men, they wash his body with water and lime.

They wrap him in white cloth, in many layers. His face is pale and waxy-looking. His mother and father and his sisters pray. Their arms are folded, right hand on left—the same way Adam's hands are folded.

His mother and father look tired.

People have been pressuring them to apologize. "You've raised a tomboy and a liberal!" they say. "Please try to be a bit ashamed."

"What Adam did, he has already done," his father says.

"We won't apologize," his mother says. "He was our son."

By the grave-side the hecklers and online hate are muted. It is quiet. There is a frangipani tree scattering its flowers—already rotting—onto the headstones and shoveled earth.

"Hello," Ghaf says. He leans against the wall by the mosque gate. He wears a smile, seemingly sympathetic.

So I ask him: "Why are you here?"

"To pay my respects," he says. "I grew up with Dyana. I was her friend."

"Adam was what his name was, you asshole. You stopped being his friend long ago. How could've you ever been his friend, you can't even call him by his name."

Ghaf shakes his head. "It is sad for her to have died in sin," he says. "I wanted to tell you, professional to professional. For our history campaign to commemorate Merdeka month, we'll use the White Mask's stenciled mural of the Tun Doctor.

"We've already discussed it with the Ministry," he says. "They agree, it's a good place for us to start, a good lesson. This way at least Dyana will have done something good in the world."

That night I leave my car in the emergency lane and walk through the underpass. I look up at the highway wall.

It's the first time I'm here in person.

The street lamps cast light at an angle. The wall is slightly rough. There is rubbish at the Tun Doctor's feet, leftovers of the police investigation—three soda cups, a blue medical glove, shreds of black bin-liner stuck in cracks between the curbstones.

The Tun Doctor looks directly at me: cheeks and jowls sagging, eyes squinting, smiling.

"Hello, you," I say. I am wearing Adam's white mask.

Sitting cross-legged, I wire electrodes to the wall. My diagnostic runs through the data. It tells me almost immediately the reason why Adam wasn't recognized as a user: a missing closing chevron bracket, early on—

A forgot-to-add-an-end-tag kind of stupid mistake.

But that's not why I'm here.

I stand down the Tun Doctor's defenses. I open my satchel of art supplies. I have a stencil with me, in eight cardboard sheets, crinkled and inexpertly cut. I tape them up.

I shake my can of smart acrylic lacquer: clickity-clack-clack-clack. Then it sputters and hisses—

And after a while there is a stenciled mural of the White Mask on the wall: arms apart, palms open; the mask in the hoodie an oval outline of the white undercoat underneath, with wet licks of black denoting grinning lips and nose and eye-holes.

The paint begins to dribble, like tears. I've sprayed too much paint on—I'm not used to the mask, it is hard to see. Art was always Adam's thing.

I am better at programming.

With my tablet editor and pen stylus I pull the White Mask's arms towards the Tun Doctor, over the Tun Doctor's shoulder. And the Tun Doctor's arm I put over the White Mask's shoulder. I push the two figures together.

Each still has a hand free. I ball their open palms into fists, and I position these in front, making them meet in the middle, touching knuckle-to-knuckle.

So now they are arm-in-arm, side by side, the White Mask and the Tun Doctor, brothers—

Fist-bumping.

I lock the pose into place. From my tablet I strip the smart paint of restraints: no lines of code asterisked out in those millions of nano-processors. All safeguards deployed. Full security.

Finally I scramble the permissions list. Not even root-access users will be able to tamper with my painting, now. The wires I've stuck to the wall spark—pak-pak!—and the electrodes fall off, shorted.

The next morning, through sunrise haze, calls to prayer bounce off the buildings:

Condominiums, shophouse rows and onion domes; a shopping mall swarmed with birds of neon-green; an office tower venting steam, its face a moving mural, a tumbling puzzle of octagons interlocking.

Joggers on zebra crossings. Stroboscopic graffiti by the riverside. A helicopter. And soon the roads are busy: a train of cars forming in every lane, red rear-lights shimmering.

In the air, people speaking—the dull murmur of social media.

"There are two White Masks, maybe?" somebody asks, and somebody else replies: "Maybe it's a conspiracy."

A third somebody says: "This is still a thing? These mural artists, they are so wanky, think they are so important. Please, people. Stop. I'm so bored of it already."

There, at the highway wall, the Terror Thursday crew stands in a semicircle.

In my online self I watch Ghaf watching the surveillance feed—

Of the White Mask between pools of street lamp light, wearing black skinny jeans and black sneakers, working. He puts cardboard stencils up in eight parts, and shakes his spray can: clickity-clack-clack-clack.

The footage fast-forwards. His arms are a blur. They slow down again only as he steps back. I admire what he's done: the White Mask and the Tun Doctor, arm-in-arm, together.

It doesn't look that bad, now that I can see it in sunlight.

"It was that tomboy's programmer bitch who did this," one of them says. And another one says: "Can't even turn the paint off. We won't be able to work like this."

Ghaf's crew is ready to work.

They have rolls of tape on their wrists, a pallet of paint tins in their parked flatbed. But there's an upended box of spray cans by the wall, and a smashed-up laptop also—its two halves cracked apart, keys scattered, screen flaked in shards.

Ghaf wipes his head. The others keep well away. Carefully, carefully, he creeps forward. He stretches his hand out.

Straightaway the Tun Doctor reacts—

With flailing whip-arms of viscous matter: reaching out, toppling cans and roller poles, flinging curbstones. Grabbing Ghaf under his shoulder.

"No-no-no!" he says, screaming.

The rest rush to drag him away. Adam, on the wall—for now, he is safe in the arms of his new best buddy. He stares down at Ghaf and the Terror Thursdays, smiling.

And—wait, no, it must be a glitch—but I see his mask has a hint of teeth showing.

Extracts from DMZINE #13 [January 2115]

FOO SEK HAN

EDITORIAL

Hanif bin Abdullah Elsyaff, Editor-in-Chief

The first DMZine of 2115 welcomes you to a new year of old beginnings. Despite the many joys and tragedies befalling the DMZ in 2114, and the great technological advances smuggled into the city, the familiar still comes to us as, well, familiar. Walking down the Pudu Pasar, the hottest music broadcasted to our consciousness is still P. Ramlee on vocaloid, infecting our dreams with the pervasive dances of a Japanese anime-inspired Mr. Ramlee with pink-green hair. Helicopters of the Ruling Party continue to scour our atmosphere, unable to find a place to land. Sometimes they still try to broadcast propaganda through the floating JAKIMechs, but even the most impressionable find the messages obsolete. Nobody pays any mind to the JAKIMechs save during prayer times, when they still drone on our airwaves faint, calming verses.

2 January marks the 10th anniversary of the ceasefire of the KL Crisis. For the benefit of younger readers, you should know that the DMZ was very different in its heyday. Before hostilities broke out in Kuala Lumpur, this used to be the economic and social hub of Malaysia. Now the Emergency States (previously known as Petaling Jaya) are taken up by the Ruling Party, and the Secessionists have claimed Kota Bharu as their own financial headquarters. The Ruling Party still controls Putrajaya, a sore point for the Secessionists

despite their control of most of the East Coast. The latest feeds from the Ruling Party's emergencycloud suggest that the Secessionist Shariah Council has finally implemented their long-in-the-making hudud laws, although it remains to be seen how many amendments post-implementation they will make—last we heard, nobody seems to agree whether heterosexual sodomy should be criminalized.

The early years of the DMZ were a great challenge to all of us. For the remaining residents in this stretch of Kuala Lumpur, in between the Mile-High Walls and Ground Zero, the formal ceasefire between the two is little consolation. The realities of the war are still ever-present: looters, hidden snipers, child suicide bombers, block-wide brainscan shutdowns remain our daily lives.

But we persevere. Tan Boo Hong aside, the DMZ of 2114 is a stabilized city, emerging as a rising state in Southeast Asia in both economy and—as when such a renaissance occurs—art and culture. The fact that this magazine continues to flourish is evidence enough of such achievement. It is said complacency is the enemy of success, and we shall not let that destroy us, or the DMZ.

Once again, younger minds may enquire: what does the DMZ mean? The global term is, of course, a Demilitarized Zone, where the laws of neither the Ruling Party nor the Secessionists can lay claim upon us. The truth is that DM stands for the Mile-High Walls—the Dataran Merdeka, where the first brainscan shutdown attack by the Secessionists happened, during that Independence Concert of the Ruling

Party of 2098. We were not sufficiently advanced at the time to avoid the use of nuclear cells for such attacks, and that is why the Ruling Party built the Walls to keep out the radiation. It is said that even now, the bodies inside are perfectly preserved.

And now I anticipate your next question. What about the Z? The truth is, nobody knows. Dull military convention dictates that it means "Zone". A journalist I met told me it should be "Zombi", for are we not all zombies, un-lifes held back by societal norms and tradition? Very poetic, but hardly persuasive. An imam claims it is "Zakat", and the DMZ is the price we pay to atone for our sins. Then at Brickfields, I have heard several professionals claim it just boils down to raw, animalistic wants and cravings of the human race—the "Zakar".

Enough about the city: let us talk about the history of this magazine. Two years ago, it would have been unthinkable to see print media flourish especially in the DMZ. Everyone was just getting information into their consciousness, whether they wanted it or not, and paper was so scarce there was little reason to use it. I still recall the day when I walked out of the Bar Council library with a copy of the defunct Ruling Party's Annotated Constitution. I sat reading it at a mamak stall, and I observed a boy staring at me from across the street. Finally, he walked over and asked if he could touch it.

"Is this what they are like?" he asked. "Books?"

But like all things old, paper is once again enjoying a revived renaissance. How is it that only after so many years, we have discovered paper to be the best way to hide information from probes and hacks? Aesthetics too play a part, in addition to practicality—it is one of the few ways digitization is not required to transfer information from one human being to another.

DMZine is blessed to have the bravest and most creative people of the DMZ as part of its collaboration. 12 months of the year of 2114, day in and day out, these people ran through the darkest corners of the DMZ and its deepclouds to give you the best and the latest in art and culture. None of us were sure if we would ever reach Issue #13, and yet, here we are. And for that, we want to thank you, dear reader, for giving us the greatest pleasure of creating this magazine every month.

To another year!

INBOX: YOUR VOICE

Our Heritage

Thank you, Alfred Kanagasamy, for your story on the fading kopitiams of the DMZ. It's sad that these places are disappearing, not just because of the KL Crisis, but also out of apathy. I was so emo remembering my dad bringing me to OldTown for their premixed coffees and freshly microwaved nasi lemaks. Granted, the food inspires little sympathy, but the style is a legacy worth remembering. *Jonathan T.*

In Memoriam

The family of Tan Boo Hong extends its thanks to the editorial team of DMZine for their moving eulogy of our dearly departed father, husband, brother and son in its 12th issue.

We Still Receive This Message on a Weekly Basis; Please Stop

Don't categorize your Games section as "Hikikomori" as it is offensive to gamer culture. "*xxTaliSeduceRxx*".

CORRECTIONS AND CLARIFICATIONS

The advertorial of Emporium Sukaria Pak Zam on Page 18 of Issue #10 should read "fun explosive kinetic toys", and not "boys". Founder Zam bin Rahim does not, and will not, entertain any request for services or goods he considers inappropriate for his establishment.

An interview in Issue #10 with Chiam Yu Shung and Michelin Liu, vintage physical memorabilia collectors who navigate the Tower 2 Ruins, misidentified the character from the 2000s animated series "Ipin dan Upin", of which the 1st edition fabric doll was Chiam and Liu's greatest achievement. The doll is Upin, the elder identical twin brother, and not Ipin, the younger identical twin brother.

The Food column of Issue #12 entitled *Tempting Thosai*, featuring an interview with head chef Dee A/L Nahendran, had incorrectly identified Dee as trans male. Dee has gently clarified to us its disassociation with the binarization of genders, and we apologize for this error. Creating each issue of DMZine is a learning process, and we strive to continue our effort to understand, accept and support all beliefs and identities in the DMZ.

PUBLIC SERVICE ANNOUNCEMENT

The break-in on 22 November at yet another abandoned Secessionist bunker at Bukit Nanas has been linked to the appearance of a strain of intelligent sociopathic dogs gathered near the area. They currently occupy the Hutan Simpan of Bukit Nanas. Recent developments of the dogs distributing Maoist propaganda suggest they may have evolved to adopt communism.

Though the intelligent sociopathic socialist dogs are known to be unfriendly but nonviolent, there have been reports of them shaking tails and requesting pettings as a lure to steal cybernetics from unsuspecting trekkers. Exercise caution when engaging the dogs, and at no point should you remind them no human society has ever successfully embraced perfect Marxism.

FOOD & DRINK

A Glimpse of the Himalayas

Introducing the Himalayan, located at the old Burger King of Masjid Jamek. Words by ***Aloysius Gill.***

This foodie was invited for a sneak preview at a soft launch earlier in December of Chef Chankrisna Maung's latest venture. In this gorgeous food temple, once the ruins of a terrible American fast food chain, vegan dishes reign supreme. The Himalayan presents fusion dishes like Burmese laphet doke, a fascinating salad of pickled tea leaves adorned with crushed fried peas and shredded spinach.

I have had the pleasure of witnessing Maung, an apprentice cook in Penang pre-KL Crisis, evolve from cooking copycat Hokkien noodles to his current unique Burmese-Nepalese cuisine with a hint of South Indian flavors. His uthappams remain some of the best pancakes I have had in this city, and coupled with fresh ingredients grown in the basement of the Himalayan, are just absolutely delectable. Sprouts and fungi grow amazingly well in the dark, as he would attest. Mushroom wine, which goes down smooth with ginger salads (a recipe by Chef Maung reproduced below for our loyal readers), is going to be the hit of 2115, mark my words.

Customers may eat on the ground floor, or in the basement with the plants. Maung is happy to accept payment in the form of manual labor in his garden.

Gyin Thoke Recipe

Serves 2-4

1 cup pickled ginger (sliced and shredded)

½ cup soybeans (roasted or fried)

½ cup pumpkin seeds

½ cup white sesame seeds (roasted)

1 cup shredded cabbage

¼ cup shallot (fried)

2 kaffir lime leaves (finely chopped)

¼ cup coriander (finely chopped)

1 cup young spinach leaves (finely sliced)

Vinaigrette

2 tbsp fresh lime juice

2 tbsp shallot oil

1 tbsp fish sauce

salt to taste

Optional

400g melon flesh (deseeded and cubed)

100g cucumber (peeled, halved and deseeded, cut into cubes)

400g kampung chicken breast (poached and shredded)

Instructions

Place all vegetables, including optional vegetables, into a mixing bowl. In another bowl, whisk vinaigrette ingredients until emulsified. Toss dressing with salad, top with shredded chicken, and serve immediately.

Health Note

Consuming non-synthetic emulsified chicken gel may have long-term cancerous effects. For optimal meatless quality, consider replacing with fried tofu.

REMEMBRANCE

The Bar Council will be leading memorial services for the 10-year anniversary of the end of the KL Crisis and the declaration of the DMZ, at Ground Zero on 2 January, 8:00pm. A ceasefire has been requested for during that time and no violence shall be tolerated. Attendees are to convene at 7:30pm at Tower 1 Survived, to walk around Tower 2 Ruins and leave candles by the Frozen Fountain. Volunteer medical professionals will be stationed to assist the elderly and the disabled.

The braincloud booth in the Bar Council building for visitors to record their messages for Tan Boo Hong will be open past 5:00pm to 12:00 midnight on 2 January.

SPIRITUALITY

Is Our Predestination Wrong?

The influence of the Brand New Kelak, clothed in their impossibly snow white robes and led by the enigmatic Karen Sukhbir, continues to evolve across the DMZ. Words by ***Jennifer Tze****.*

"My name is Karen Sukhbir, and I am from the future."

Thus begins my introduction to the enigmatic leader of the Brand New Kelak, the latest spirituality movement born in the DMZ. In person, Ms. Sukhbir is dressed in a plain white sari, and her smile is guileless—almost to a fault. It is surprising to me that a 19-year-old girl can be so calm and relaxed, especially as she is leading an evening mass of at least 200 people.

The members of the movement—they refuse to call themselves a religion—are equally as disarming as Karen. They carry themselves plainly, dressed in normal everyday clothes. There are no insignias, no totems, not even a figurine. There are no books of commandments, nor scrolls of dead oceans.

I sit through the evening mass, and I am surprised—once more—by how simple Karen's sermons are. I had been expecting prayers biodelivered to our consciousness, or tacky holographics of her "future".

Instead, she starts with a simple question: *Do you believe in yourself?* Most of the congregation shake their heads.

"There are some days I don't," she says. "But I think of all the people who look up to me, and I make myself stronger." She gives a casual grin. "People like you."

The congregation cheers, then smiles quietly. Karen continues, extolling the virtues of common sense prevailing over fanaticism, playing a guitar, then leading exercises encouraging us to laugh, then cry hysterically (the latter is, admittedly, pretty weird). We hug each other for minutes. In the end, a member rolls out a karaoke deck, and she sings to the crowd ancient Awie tunes.

Of course, what is a spiritual movement without its idiosyncrasies? In between the singing and crying, she answers questions about her "future".

"Time, in its greatest arrogance," Karen tells us, "has determined the future for mankind, and we are creatures of fate rather than choice. We need to make it parallel to all dimensions, rather than orthogonal."

The people of Karen's future have discovered this principle of predestination, and they sent her back in time to create a "temporal space-time anamolic scar" to give us all the chance to change our lives.

"This is a movement," she says softly. "Ultimately, we will save mankind. I know we will. I know you will."

No, she answers a disappointed member, there are no jetpacks in the future.

As the session closes, I still remain unmoved, though a little less certain. Karen does not disclose any war or devastation in the future—or at least, nothing worse than the

KL Crisis. Is she saving us from a future of ruin, or rather, a boring tomorrow?

A fellow member helps me pack my things, and I chance a question. "Those people who sent Karen back from the future. Do you think Time played a hand in making them send her?"

He passes me my coat. "I'm sure the future people considered that."

Membership (free) is open for all people at the north wing of the Oriental Folk Music Center at all hours. Ask for Mrs. Soon, Leah or Omar.

7 THINGS TO DO IN THE DMZ

Comedy

Farukh "Harith ISISkandar" Mokhtar is back…now with even more Eyebots (or as he calls them, his ISISbots!) to bring us the most stomach-churning news of the Emergency States! Farukh will be performing his crowd-pleasing crazy headlines recitation routine. Mon-Sat nightly Live@Kelab DiRaja Selangor.

Music

After significant renovations, Mr. Soon Yee Fung has reopened the Oriental Folk Music Center, though only the south wing is accessible. With the north wing closed, the space is now much more compact, although enhanced security means a permanent SkinMelt™ screen has been set up in the middle of the Center. Mrs. Soon's erhu lessons are discontinued until further notice.

Dance

Revered dancer Rashid Teoh will be performing in the Dewan Filharmonik Petronas Sime Darby classic works of Tchaikovsky and Stravinsky, re-envisioned to incorporate tales of the Ramayana paired with Bay-era *Transformers*. Richard Hay of the Displaced Philharmonic Orchestra conducts this magical yet progressive work. 22-24 January.

Party

The newest dance floor of KoozhOut is now open in the former KWSP building! Thursdays are Salaryman Nights—get in your best business suit and high heels and dance the night away to synthwave, surrounded by hopelessly outdated Ruling Party computers! All substances worthy of abuse can be purchased at the entrance.

Note: By consuming and/or substituting your limbs and organs with any abuse-worthy substances, you indefinitely indemnify and hold harmless KoozhOut of all liabilities.

Shop

Deliciously daredevil fashionista Yasmine Khaiira is back in town. This time, her Liquid Sky electroclash wear is sourced from abandoned wardrobes of the Mandarin Oriental, and Levels 3 and 4 of Tower 2 Ruins. Catch her stall in the middle of the Sunday Pasar Pagi at Pudu Row. Be quick—stock runs out fast.

Synthethasia

The stars are brihgt tonight. Fuel Cells, Middle Eastern retrocraze, smuggle into DMZ complete. Vendor information not available. Vendor information not availazxxxxxbatch 00x23401710837g08zh014 <<MACHINE CODE UNINTL3LIGIBLE>> Lihgt p safe,

Art

Rogue graffiti artist Tida'Apa has put up an installation on the Mile-High Walls, "The Bike Messenger", as a tribute to Tan Boo Hong. The biodegradable nature of the exhibitions means unpredictable fluctuations in the art, and repeat visits are encouraged. New to the Tida'Apa phenomenon? Pre-configured cryptographic code in the graffiti can cancel out any camera feature in your devices or synthetic eyes, and taking pictures without permission may result in blindness.

X

PULP FICTION

Level Up 2014: Part 2 of 7

In the far-flung post-apocalyptic nuclear future of 2014, the Seven-Decade Android War is a thing of the past…or is it? Last month, Jae-Won infiltrated the Cyberjaya Multimedia Institute and came face to face with Dato' Badak, and his team of bodyguards—including the beautiful Ayesha. Curated and reproduced by ***Acts in Motion.***

Impossible! Jae-Won is furious. How can Ayesha, the legendary assassin of Miri, be a lackey to the nefarious Dato' Badak?

As if hearing his thoughts, Ayesha grins and unsheathes her Hanzo electrokatana. The red eyes behind her Cyberview shades twinkle and blink. "It is time for you to die, vagrant," she cries. "For I am part woman, part machine, and all Strong Female Antagonist!"

"Hur hur hur hur hur," Dato' Badak laughs his evil laugh. A purple streak of lightning flashes in the background, and his face is for one moment illuminated. He adjusts his glasses and hisses at Jae-Won. "Take him out, my gorgeous Badak's angel!"

Before Jae-Won can react, Ayesha flips herself over Dato' Badak's desk, doing a triple somersault. He barely dodges the high heels of her leather boots, which graze his chin. Blood flows out; he rubs it with the back of his mechanical hand and tastes the cast-iron cells in his white android blood.

For one moment, she falters. But she immediately lunges at Jae-Won with her electrokatana. He quickly tumbles back, and releases from within the sleeves of his vintage varsity jacket his twin lightkerises. Ayesha swings her blade against him, and Jae-Won blocks it with the kerises, causing sparks and virtual cherry blossoms to fly and burn little holes in the carpets of Dato' Badak's office.

"You and I are the same, Ayesha!" he cries. "Remember our code of honor. Do not submit to this fleshy fool!"

It is only then he sees the red eyes of Ayesha: the coding inside...someone has tampered with it!

"You reprogrammed her!" Jae-Won yells. "In clear defiance of the Human-Android Treaty of 2000...what you do could prompt another apocalypse!"

"Hur hur hur hur," Dato' Badak laughs again. He raises his right hand, palm up, to reveal a black rectangular box with a large red button. "See for yourself what wonders I have!"

Jae-Won gasps. "The Internet!" he yells with unmatched robotic wrath. "You have taken the World Wide Web hostage!"

"Plundered from the demagnetized hands of Stephen Hawking himself!" Another thunderous bolt of lightning, this time pink, flashes in the dark. Dato' Badak laughs menacingly. "And I shall use it for money and power!"

Jae-Won wards off another swing from Ayesha's electric sword, and deftly kicks her at the side. She falls to the ground.

"You think just because you've got the power, you'll have the touch?" Jae-Won chastizes Dato' Badak. "If anything were to happen to it, society will tear itself apart, like an angry child with a napkin!" If he has the Internet, there is no telling what evil he can unleash upon the post-apocalyptic future of 2014!

"You want to take it to the limit then?" Dato' Badak hollers. He pulls out from his pocket a glowing ball, which Jae-Won recognizes instantly: a B.O.M.B (Ballistic-Operative Malpurposive Bedlam)! "Since I'm racist against Artificial Sapiens, both of you can die! Hur hur hur!"

He arms the B.O.M.B. and hurls it against Ayesha. Jae-Won, against his own mechanical instincts, lets his human side take control. He bionic sprints towards Ayesha and grabs her to his chest, then jumps through the glass windows. As they fall the B.O.M.B. explodes, and the last thing he remembers is Ayesha's questioning eyes, as the shock reprograms her to her default android state…

To be continued.

HIKIKOMORI
Epilogues
Studio Insaf

Another month, another walking simulator. Epilogues is a visual graphic novel featuring the DMZ, which sounds like every other DMZ game out there except for one twist: you play a Tentera Darat of the Ruling Party in the first year of the KL Crisis. Supposedly based on a journal found by the developers, gamers may be surprised by the use of archaic, PC-unfriendly words such as "Islamist" and "kafir". The beautiful environments produced by Studio Insaf, accompanied by strings of the late Raina Shah, make Epilogues a great experience for its short campaign length. One minor fault: Epilogues's attempt to be art by questioning the reality of games is extremely telegraphed and can be seen as preachy. 7/10

Mass Murder Simulator

Dislike Productions

The long-awaited spiritual sequel to Serial Killer Simulator is fan-panderingly gruesome, featuring an unlikable protagonist whose motivations are limited to "kill everyone because I don't like everyone". Any semblance of nuance is thrown out of the window, and the developers have themselves claimed they are "anti-art games". Running on the same engine as SKS, the animation appears dated, and the graphic deaths are, thankfully for this reviewer, cartoonish at best. 4/10

Editor's Note: As at the date of publication, Dislike Productions will be uploading patches to remove Ruling Party militant models and dialogue alluding to torture of DMZ citizens.

PEOPLE

Suraya bt Mohd Nur, 19, Bicycle Courier

What do you do?

I ride bikes.

Any specifics?

Hantar shit for anyone who pays.

Do you worry about Ruling Party militants, after what happened?

Sucks. But shit still needs hantaring.

Any last thoughts?

Yeah, RIP.

Jarvinder Singh, 60, Nursery Owner

What do you do?

I planted vegetables in the balcony before the KL Crisis. They didn't survive, and once it all settled down I thought, why not? We still have soil, seeds can be sourced both inside and out, and I still have my hands. Synthetic veg taste like shit anyway. Found whole apartments empty and stripped clean by looters, so I just did the same thing as at my balcony, just big scale.

What kind of vegetables?

The usual: kangkung, onions, ginger, sprouts. Cili padi, of course. Most important of them all.

Your greatest success?

Discovering bamboo. Those things grow fast. The subthermal bomb the Secessionists used on the Ground Zero park actually made conditions perfect. Now we can build houses with them, burn them for warmth, even pulp them to make paper like for your magazine.

"Alif", Age Unknown, Underground Hacker

What do you do?

who r u?

Are you in the middle of an operation?

who is this

I won't tell.

?? how did you locate this privatecloud

I've been a fan and [Interview ended upon cloud shutdown. Subsequent login attempts failed.]

Zacked Hon, 34, Tattoo Artist/Aquarium Keeper

What do you do?

Got my own parlor at the Aquaria right by the jellyfishes. Best view in town.

What's your favorite work?

Getting the dolphins to talk to us on the brainscan module again. Took some persuading. Claimed they were just entertaining us 'cause of the fish but I know them. They like me.

How about the tattoos?

This Japanese chick made me draw a whole garden on her back. Claims it's a treasure map of some kind. Got her some modular ink to make the grass shake when it rains, and the clouds move when there's wind. Should have taken a hologram.

Any weird requests?

Some dude wanted me to draw on his butt… get this. Mermen dressed up like militia, shirts open, clean-shaven and white teeth. Wanted the fish tails in glittering ink. The dolphins said it's sick, but I'm teaching them tolerance these days.

Suraya bt Mohd Nur (Addendum)

You wanted to tell us more?

I'm bad with words. But I got to say this.

We couriers, we got a code: never ask. We just collect the package, send it to the target, collect the trade, go home.

Hong was one of our best. He never asked, just smiled and did the job. I saw the surveillancecloud feeds. He went into Tower 1 Survived top floor, never knew it was full of Ruling Party militants. Never checked that the package was from the Secessionists. He's just a delivery boy.

The Emergency States, they say he threw himself out, like some mental out of his brains on Koozhshit. But I saw the feeds. The bamboo strips filed under the nails, the pliers on the teeth…shit. I'm sorry.

Oh my god, I'm so sorry. I'm messing up.

I want to send a message.

We're coming for them.

You can't do this.

Why the fuck not? So what they did to Hong, that's fine, then?

It's not.

Then don't stand in my way. You're just some entertainment journalist, you're not on the ground. You don't know what we know.

What you're suggesting may rock whatever peace the DMZ—

Fuck you.

Someone died. Someone fucking died.

That guy who died is my friend.

If the peace we have means I need to let my friend die in vain, then fuck you. Fuck them, too.

We're coming. All of us. The dogs too.

[Interview ended with Suraya riding away. Repeated attempts to continue interview were unsuccessful.]

Editor's Note: The views expressed by interviewees do not necessarily represent the views of, and should not be attributed to, DMZine.

BIOS

×

Zen Cho was born and raised in Selangor, and lives in London. She is the author of Crawford Award-winning short story collection *Spirits Abroad*, also published by Fixi Novo. Her debut novel is *Sorcerer to the Crown*, the first of a historical fantasy trilogy published by Ace/Roc Books (US) and Pan Macmillan (UK). Find out more about her work at http://zencho.org.

Angeline Woon is a Malaysian writer who resides in Canada. Her stories are in the *Esquire* magazine, the *KL Noir: White*, *Readings from Readings 2* and *FUTURA* anthologies, have been read on BFM Radio, and performed at klpac, Love Art Labs' *Ecosexual White Wedding to Snow* and Nuit Blanche Ottawa.

Anna Tan loves dancing around words and pretending to know how to dance. In real life, Anna makes a living annoying other bean counters by sniffing out their dirty sox. www.annatsp.com.

Sharmilla Ganesan is a features writer with an English-language newspaper. She enjoys telling stories: to humans, robots and everyone in between.

Terence Toh writes newspaper and magazine articles by day, and fiction by night. He is a merry wanderer of the night, constantly searching the world for fulfilment, inspiration and affordable plates of pasta. His short plays have been performed at the Short and Sweet Theatre and Musical festivals in Kuala Lumpur and Penang. Most recently, his short stories have been featured in anthologies such as *KL Noir: White*, *Amok* and *Allusions of Innocence.*

Rafil Elyas licked a lot of 9V batteries in his childhood and became interested in science. He currently specializes in using mathematical modeling and simulation for the design, optimization and troubleshooting of hydrocarbon production and processing facilities. He also fronts satire punk band The Panda Head Curry? and writes short stories.

Ted Mahsun grew up a Muslim but was turned into a robot, slaved to the system. In an attempt to break free, he writes speculative fiction, which is a fancy way to say he spends his time lazing about dreaming and not contributing anything worthwhile to society.

William Tham Wai Liang was once a cherry genome analyst on an isolated hilltop research station. He analysed cherries and also wrote and published a story called *Kakak*.

Kris Williamson is the director of Literary Concept. He is the editor of *Anak Sastra* literary magazine and has published short fiction, travel narratives, and poetry. His first novel, *Son Complex*, was published by Fixi Novo in 2013. He can be stalked at kriswilliamson.com or on Twitter at @iramalama.

Adiwijaya Iskandar started writing plays in 2008, winning best script in the 2009 Short and Sweet festival and staging his first full length play, *Rancangan Harijadi Terhebat Adli*, in 2010. He is now venturing into prose fiction.

Chin Ai-May loves to tell lies for fun and profit. She was published in *KL Noir: Yellow* (Fixi Novo, 2014) and on The Calistro Prize 2014 shortlist for her YA novella. Born and bred in Petaling Jaya, she spends her days reading, 'riting and avoiding 'rithmetic.

After two decades in the legal industry, Syamsuriatina Ishak or **Tina Isaacs** as her friends know her, decided to share her myriad experiences and observations by resuming her love for fiction writing. She is presently pursuing an MFA in Creative Writing in Tampa, Florida and working on her debut novel.

Tariq Kamal is a short story author, and *Unusual Suspects* is his first published work (everything else being blogs, college newsletters and fan fiction). These days, he balances his time between his day job in the IT industry and his family, and lives with his wife and children in Petaling Jaya.

Zedeck Siew used to work in media, for publications like *Kakiseni*, *The Nut Graph*, and *Poskod.my*. As part of CENTAUR he co-designed POLITIKO, a card game about Malaysian party politics. He is currently working on his first book, an illustrated catalog of imaginary Southeast Asian animals.

Foo Sek Han is a legal professional in Kuala Lumpur whose legal and creative writings have appeared on the *Sun*, *KL Noir: Yellow*, *Esquire Malaysia* and a Media Law book published by Sweet & Maxwell Asia. His cyberpunk knowledge is restricted to acting in a wedding video.

FIXI.COM.MY